Hope this makes you laugh!

Andrew

REMY'S DILEMMA

by Andrew Snook

Illustrations and cover art by Pj Monfero

 **FriesenPress**

Suite 300 - 990 Fort St
Victoria, BC, Canada, V8V 3K2
www.friesenpress.com

ISBN
978-1-4602-6275-7 (Hardcover)
978-1-4602-6276-4 (Paperback)
978-1-4602-6277-1 (eBook)

1. Fiction, Humorous

Distributed to the trade by The Ingram Book Company

For my one true love, Cristine.

REMY'S DILEMMA

I

awakenings

It started with a dream, or at least what I thought was a dream. I know now it was a premonition, a sneak peek into the destruction of my world. It appeared in the form of a powerful whisper across the airwaves. The voice, humanity's reaper, was hidden deep inside the hollowed belly of a rocky beast in Colorado. As it spoke, our time on this planet was given an expiration date.

"My fellow Glamericans, we are under attack from the terrorist organization known as Nations Against Glomitrox. Several nations with direct ties to N.A.G. have begun fuelling weapons of mass destruction, which they intend to fire on our country if I do not surrender myself for alleged crimes against humanity. Do not believe their propaganda.

Our nuclear strikes on Paris, Moscow, Hong Kong, Tokyo, Berlin and Rome were pre-emptive strikes meant to protect the Glamerican people. We were completely within our rights to defend our homeland — especially after the underhanded assault on the City of Regina by unknown assailants that claimed thousands of lives. This unwarranted aggression will not go unchecked.

Any nation that supports the terrorist activities of N.A.G. should consider this broadcast a final warning. Glamerica demands that all countries cease any plans for hostile actions against our fine state, or we will have no choice but to launch a full nuclear strike on all non-Glamerican soil.

Any Glamericans trained on how to survive a nuclear strike are to go door-to-door immediately and show their fellow citizens how to properly hide under a desk.

This is Prime Minister Harper Day signing off. Good night and Glam bless."

I sat up and sprang from my bed, drenched in perspiration from the combination of my dream and the hot, humid July night. My chest felt tight, making it hard to breathe. My heart was racing. I ran outside onto my balcony for some fresh air. Pulling a cigarette from a pack of Cats that had been sitting on my windowsill, I took a few puffs and began to calm down. I took a moment to check out my view of Mississauga's east end, which was comprised of nothing but other old, run-down high-rise apartment buildings and abandoned factories. This area of the city has seen better days.

Remembering my dream, I snapped back into a panic, dropped my cigarette, and ran to my bedroom closet. Opening the closet door unleashed a tidal wave of garbage and old knick-knacks. I frantically rummaged through my belongings, searching for a promise. After a few anxious minutes, I found my orange Hungry Boy lunchbox, held it to my right ear and shook it intensely. The sound of rattling filled my ear. Oh, thank God!

If you knew the end of the world was coming, how would you spend the time you had left? Would you try and right a lifetime of wrongs, repent your sins, and attempt to secure a spot in the land of your almighty? Would you seek out family members to remember the better days or rebuild relationships lost long ago?

I suppose these options create closure for some people, I'm just not one of them. However, I found a path that is equally fulfilling, at least in the short-term, which suits me just fine. After all, it's not like having long-term goals makes much sense now, anyway. My name is Remy Delemme, and my world is going to die.

* * * *

In downtown Toronto's financial district, detective Tobias Gray awoke from his slumber at 6 a.m. in his three-bedroom luxury condominium.

Gray sat up in his king-sized bed and stretched his arms towards the ceiling before getting up to start his day. He neatly tucked the top sheet under the mattress before placing the comforter back on his bed, making it look like it had never been slept in. He then made his way to the bathroom, where he shaved while listening to the hisses from the automatic coffee maker in his kitchen as it slowly dripped into a travel mug. He opened his bedroom closet and removed a tweed jacket, a well-ironed black turtleneck, a neatly folded pair of blue jeans, briefs and black knit socks, and got dressed. He then slipped his weapon holster on, which housed a 9mm semi-automatic pistol, and strapped his backup, Betty — a lightweight, five-shot, snubnose revolver — around his ankle. After combing his black hair, neatly parting it to the right side, he headed down the hall towards the kitchen.

Gray grabbed a pen and crossed off a box on the calendar attached to his fridge. Today is Thursday, July 11, 2041. He picked up a piece of paper, opened his fridge and made a list: *Bread, Milk, Eggs, Chicken, Potatoes, Peanut butter.*

Picking up his travel mug, he took a sip while watching the sun rise over his thriving neighbourhood. He let out a deep, satisfied breath.

Today is going to be a good day, he said to himself as he headed downstairs to the building's garage. Gray walked over to his blue, electric-powered Fraud Shocker, hopped in, and began his drive to Division 22 of the Toronto Police Department.

* * * *

As I tore the lid off my childhood lunchbox, my Smiley Guy stamper, a crayon and several crumpled pieces of paper fell out and scattered across the floor of my apartment. I grabbed the stamper and crayon and placed them in the pocket of the jeans I was still wearing from the night before. I often slept in my clothes on Wednesday nights. Wednesday had become a regular drinking night for me, and taking off your clothes when you're drunk is just too complicated, especially when belts and socks are involved. I looked over at the clock, forgetting that its hands had been stuck at 1:45 a.m. for more than a month. Not that it really mattered. Waking up at random hours in a daze has never been a conflict for me since I don't believe it's necessary to have steady employment.

I opened each piece of paper, tossing them aside until I found a letter labelled, "Things To Do Today."

It was written in irradiated emerald green crayon, my favourite colour in the fourth grade. As I read the contents of the letter, it transformed from a child's ramblings into the most important document I had ever possessed.

Dear Me,

If you are reading this, then you will soon be in heaven, singing with the angels.

I paused for a moment, rolling my eyes at the naiveté of my youth, and then continued reading.

Here is a list of important stuff you need to do before we grow our wings.

(#1) Get to second base

I couldn't hold back my excited, girlish giggle. A week after I wrote this letter, I made my way to second base. Rebecca Lashley. She had long, blonde hair, big, blue eyes, and a beautiful smile. Poor girl, she never even saw it coming. I can remember body checking her off second base to prevent the double play like it was yesterday. Such a wonderful childhood memory!

After I finished reminiscing, I turned my attention back to the letter and continued to scroll down the list. To my horror, I realized the first item was the only goal I ever accomplished. I still had nine quests to complete.

(#2) Go cow tipping

(#3) Own sweet ride

(#4) Become one with nature

(#5) Go hunting and shoot at stuff

(#6) Try exotic cuisine

(#7) Find true love

(#8) Find the answer to man's greatest question!

(#9) Help out the elderly

(#10) Have a near-death experience

There was no way I could complete all these challenges before nuclear Armageddon arrived on my doorstep, so I decided to focus on the goal that plagued me to this day — finding the answer to man's greatest question! The remaining goals would have to be placed on the backburner.

Knowing there was no time to waste, I began preparing myself for the road ahead. Who knows when the first bombs will drop? Hopefully, fortune would smile upon me and grant me enough time to complete what I started so long ago.

I decided my first order of business was to gather my valuables and trade them for items I would require on my journey. If I was to live my last few days on Earth attempting to complete an important quest, I would do so with the proper equipment. Money was no longer of any value to me. The Glamerican dream for excessive waistlines and wallets was never hardwired into my brain to begin with, so I didn't think I would miss any of my worldly possessions — unlike those people who'd been changed forever by Glomitrox. It's a shame so many citizens have already forgotten the soulless monster known as Glomitrox, and how it altered the face of our nation.

Back in 2032, Americanadians suffered the biggest health-care crisis that had ever existed in their country's history. Eighty per cent of the population was diagnosed with liver cancer and ninety-five per cent of those diagnosed required transplants that were hard to obtain. Many of the nation's leaders were left dumbstruck, wondering how this could have happened. Of course, the answer was staring them in the face the entire time. It was Saskatchewan's fault.

The province's political leaders subsidized a pharmaceutical company that specialized in the production of fat- and calorie-burning diet pills, as well as artery-opening medications. The company was called Glomitrox. The resource-rich province funded the company in an effort to combat obesity problems affecting the majority of the province's youth, due to an overwhelming number of children suffering from wheat addiction.

As soon as news spread of the effectiveness of the company's medications, most Americanadians started taking them daily to avoid interrupting their gluttonous lifestyles with irritations such as heart disease or having to pay for two seats on an airplane. Unfortunately, many of them failed to take notice of the liver-related side effects written on the prescription bottles. This was probably due to the high illiteracy rate in the country at that time. The liver shortage caused the citizens of Americanada to die off at a rate not seen in the western world since the Second World War. The medical community was at a loss with how to cope with all the sick and dying, but Glomitrox knew exactly what to do.

Since it was already the most profitable and powerful company in the world, Glomitrox had a great deal of power and influence over Americanada's political leaders. So it was of little surprise to the masses when Bill-U4ME was passed in the White House of Commons with little conflict. Bill-U4ME gave Glomitrox full control of the Americanadian military, allowing it to infiltrate underdeveloped nations for the purpose of organ harvesting. Glomitrox's original plan was to clone the livers, but the company's board of directors vetoed the move, citing direct harvesting as a more cost-effective approach to the shortage. The decision passed almost unanimously.

After the destruction of several small nations, N.A.G. was formed by some of the world's most powerful nations, including Switzermany, The Republic of Chindia and Brazuela. Its purpose was to ensure the growing menace known as Glomitrox would never enter another country's borders.

When the liver scare finally ended in 2035, Glomitrox refused to give up control of the military. With an economic and military stranglehold on the continent, political leaders could do little to prevent the birth of the world's destroyer. Glamerica was born. Thanks, Saskatchewan.

The citizens of Glamerica didn't give much thought to Glomitrox taking control of the entire continent and moving the capital to Saskatoon. I guess after the five-year name dispute over what to call the merger of the United States of America and Canada (minus Quebec and New Brunswick, now an independent state known as New Quebec), the people of Glamerica simply didn't care about the name of their country any more. Besides, now that Glamerica could supply an endless number of livers to its citizens at bargain-basement prices, residents happily went back to their gluttonous lifestyles, as if the epidemic that killed eighty-three million people had never happened.

2

Cash, Credit or Crunch

The first item on my shopping list was a van. Selling all of my belongings out of a van would be much more convenient than lugging an item or two at a time into my beat-up hatchback. In addition to the convenience of moving my possessions all at once, a van would hold my mattress and be more comfortable to sleep in. After all, who doesn't enjoy falling into an intoxicated dream state on the floor of a van? I hopped into my car and began the search for my new chariot at about eight o'clock in the morning.

While scouring the streets of Old Toronto, I came across Tackyland Auto Sales at 126 Bloor Street. The car lot was aptly named — and not just because it was owned and operated by Samuel Tacky. Pink and yellow flowers decorated the outside of the old brick building. The obnoxious shine of chrome seemed to come from every direction as I drove onto the lot and parked my old, not-so-dependable friend.

I could feel a cold tingle creep up my spine. It felt like I had just entered another dimension, where every inhabitant was colour blind. It reminded me of a recurring nightmare I had as a child. I was playing in my bedroom. The walls were decorated with clouds and fighter planes. My action figures and comic books covered most of the parquet flooring. I was playing with toy soldiers when I heard a bump inside my closet. Like any curious child, I dragged my butt across the floor to investigate the noise. When I opened the closet door, a tidal wave of smiling puppets dressed in bright, ugly suits smothered me and I was helpless against them. My ears were being overwhelmed with pillow talk like "I love you," "You're my best friend," and "Let's settle down and raise a family." It felt like their demonic grins and overly cheerful voices were swallowing my soul. This car lot reminded me of that nightmare. Tackyland Auto Sales may have been my personal hell.

I felt on edge as I made my way through the car lot towards the showroom. I cautiously thought out every step I took in an attempt to avoid contact with anyone in a loud blazer and bad wig. I would only call a salesman to my side when absolutely necessary. I felt like a soldier trudging through a swampy jungle, carefully avoiding traps laid out by the enemy. Each step I made could be my last moment of privacy.

I used the vehicles outside as ground cover to narrowly avoid confrontations with greasy salesmen. I got about halfway through the lot when I was spotted by a man in a bad suit and cheap hairpiece. I panicked and looked for a place to hide. I spotted a large, rusty oil drum about fifteen feet away. Even if he saw me, there was no way he would attempt to penetrate that mighty fortress of tetanus. I lunged out from behind a vehicle and headed towards the rusty haven. The salesman spotted me, but by then he was too late. I had already climbed onto the roof of a car and launched myself towards my sanctuary. While airborne, it was as if time slowed down to the point of stopping. The sound of screams echoed in my ears for what felt like an eternity. The salesman was running towards me, yelling something I couldn't understand. What was he trying to say? Then it hit me. He was yelling "Oil."

Crapsicles!

Residents a block away couldn't help but hear my high-pitched scream as I collided with twenty-seven gallons of recycled, lumpy crude. The impact sent a tidal wave of greasy goodness directly into the ugly wig and blazer of the staff member who tried to warn me. He was less than pleased. In contrast, I felt calm. The man was no longer part of my childhood nightmare, even as he yanked me from the barrel. He was simply your average Joe covered in oil who was now kicking me in the rib cage.

"You crazy son of a bitch!" the salesman yelled. "You've ruined my suit!"

"You're ruining my ribs!" I replied from my turtle-like defensive position on the ground.

"Give me a good reason to stop!"

"I want to buy a van. Today."

The man's frown instantly turned upside down. After helping me to my feet, he attempted to casually brush the liquid gold off his yellow blazer with a pink handkerchief as he cleared his throat to begin his sales pitch.

"So, you're looking for a van, eh?" he said, while creeping into my personal space. "Well, it's a good thing old Sal spotted you before these vultures dug their claws into you," he said, referring to his co-workers, all of whom lay motionless on the showroom floor, surrounded by empty bottles of tequila. "Those people would have robbed you blind."

At this point, Sal's mouth was almost touching my ear. I could feel the spittle shoot off his reptilian tongue onto my petrified lobes. I think his saliva held venomous qualities that paralyzed potential customers' nervous systems, forcing them to stand motionless. I could really go for some of that tequila.

"Yup," Sal said. "Today is your lucky day."

Sal grabbed my hand and began dragging me around the lot, like a mother keeping close watch on her child. He introduced me to several unsightly vehicles that he referred to as "damn fine-lookin' ladies."

I have never understood why men refer to vehicles as if they were women. Perhaps most men are unable to see women as anything more than objects for their entertainment — what a sad statement on the current state of our society. My train of thought became derailed when a busty redhead with a sweet ass and luscious legs stepped out of a blue sedan parked at the far end of the lot. Sal's eyes quickly focused on the hypnotic bounce of her behind. His hormones appeared to overpower his slick sales demeanour as he blurted out, "Hey, Big Red, does your flavour last all day long?"

The woman looked in our direction. The fire in her eyes was either overwhelming passion or anger — I've never been good at reading a woman's emotional state.

"I better say something to calm the situation," I said to my oily companion. Sal nodded in response.

I tried to right the verbal wrong spoken by the salesman and save us from any future angry looks; unfortunately, my brain seemed to be inoperable as well.

"Baby, you can spank my ass and make me a sandwich anytime," I yelled.

My words calmed the woman down like a smack in the mouth. Her eyes now solely focused on me. She charged me, screaming what sounded like primal war cries. I turned to Sal to see what our plan of action should be, but he had already barricaded himself in his office, leaving behind only a trail of Texas tea. As I turned back towards my aggressor, a boot caught me square in the jaw. My head snapped back like a child's candy dispenser. I'm sure the pain would have affected me worse, but I blacked out after her mule kick to my groin.

I awoke to Sal standing over my beaten body, holding a piece of oily paper. "That chick just whooped your ass!" he said while chuckling. "You must have made a pretty good impression on her. She left you a note with her phone number. Talk about a score!"

I stared at Sal in disbelief.

"Did she really leave me her number?" I asked.

"Check it out," Sal replied as he helped me to my feet.

Sal handed me the note, grinning a grin that would have made the Marquis de Sade giggle. He was creepy.

The note read:

> *Dear moron who ruined my boots with all that oil and blood, you owe me $500. If you do not pay me I will hunt you down and remove your testicles with a claw hammer. My number is 1 (555) 555-5555. You have 24 hours.*
>
> *Kailey*

"Ha," I yelled to Sal in a triumphant tone. "All beauty and no brains, that one." I crumpled up the paper and tossed it away. "Wasting time collecting money, like any of us will be around long enough to see her spend it."

Sal stared at me for the next minute. What's his problem? Sal eventually broke the awkward silence by continuing his sales pitch as if we'd never been interrupted or covered in oil.

"I think you'll really like our new minivans," he said as he took me into the showroom.

It was difficult to decide which vehicle I would purchase to move my belongings.

"They're all so ugly and unsatisfying," I said.

"Just like my ex-wives," Sal replied, laughing. "I'm sure we can find you a nice little lady to drive out of here."

"I hope so, Sal. This is beginning to feel as unfulfilling as entering Mr. Hippy's House of Hemp and coming out with a pair of pants and some rope."

Just when I thought I would have to settle for a yellow or pink monstrosity, perfection appeared. It was a brand new silver retro-series Fraud Tortoise minivan, fully equipped with a cassette player and wood panelling.

"Now this is a primo vehicle, Sal."

"What, the retro-series? Are you pulling my leg?"

"Why? Is that anything like pulling your finger?"

"That van isn't technically for sale. We're just holding it for the factory."

"Why? It's perfect. I especially like the silver colour."

"What silver? It hasn't been painted yet."

"Sold!"

The lack of pink and yellow on the shiny, steel battlewagon practically sold itself. I had to have that van.

"Um, okay then. Let's head over to my office and we'll work out the financials."

Sal's small, square-shaped workroom was filled with the loud, obnoxious hum of an old air conditioner. It rested above his desk, which made him difficult to hear.

"Look, um… what's your name?"

"Remy."

"Look, Remy, I know you've got your mind set on driving that beauty off the lot today, but I'm going to need a significant down payment before I can let that happen."

"No problem, Sal. I haven't sold any of my possessions yet, but if you let me drive the van over to my apartment I promise to come back with my pull-out couch for you. I'll even throw in my current vehicle as part of the down payment."

Sal laughed a hearty laugh, sending his belly into an amusing little dance.

"Good one, pal," he said. "But seriously, I need to see some cash."

I would have found greater humour in Sal's jiggling, but I couldn't shut out the sound of that damn air conditioner. It was beginning to pierce my brain like a baby's scream. After Sal realized I was serious about my offer of a cushy and comfortable down payment, he jumped to his feet and began cursing at the top of his lungs while pounding his fists on the desk. The combination of Sal's obscenities and the air conditioner was beginning to give me a migraine. I hate migraines.

"Cash or credit, you deadbeat!" Sal yelled as he continued to pound on his desk. "Cash or credit!"

I closed my eyes and plugged my ears. The noise was becoming unbearable. All of a sudden, a crunch-like sound penetrated my ears and the room went silent.

I opened my eyes to see Sal slumped back in his chair with an air conditioner sitting where his head should be. A combination of blood and oil trickled down the left side of his body, where his neck appeared to have been folded in half. I guess the air conditioner wasn't attached in accordance with proper installation practices. Poor Sal. Oh well, he only missed out on a small amount of time on Earth. I guess in the big scheme of things that means he led a pretty long life.

I picked up the ownership papers from Sal's desk, quickly scribbled an IOU on a napkin and tacked it to a corkboard in his office. In the note, I advised staff to bring up the air conditioner at their next safety committee meeting and to forward Sal's commission from the sale of the van to his next of kin. I also let them know that Sal's petty cash box required a refill. I left the office with a bounce in my step. The sun felt warm and inviting. The world felt full of possibilities. I hopped into my new van and got acquainted with my chariot. As I turned the key, the van's engine responded with a glorious purr. I slammed my foot on the gas and made my way back towards my apartment to prepare for the trip.

* * * *

At 8:30 a.m. at the violent crimes division of TPD Division 22, detective Tobias Gray organizes his desk for the second time this week.

"A place for everything and everything in its place, eh, Toby?" said rookie detective John Crump.

"That's Detective Gray to you, rookie, and if you go through my desk again, I will shoot you."

"I was only looking for a stapler for my report on th—"

"I don't care if you were searching for a gun to defend us from a hungry mob of cannibals."

Crump stared back at Gray, confused by his supervising officer's last comment.

"I don't get it."

"What I'm saying is, if I only had one bullet left in my gun and there was a hungry mob of cannibals staring us down with knives and forks in hand, and you were digging through my desk to find us more bullets, I would shoot you first."

"But what about the cannibals?"

"I would offer them your carcass but warn them your ghost might go routing through their personal belongings whenever they were away."

"I still don't get it."

"Moral of the story, stay out of my desk."

Crump stood silent and nodded, knowing full well he still didn't understand why Gray brought up cannibals as a way to tell him to stay out of his stuff. Ever since being promoted to the homicide desk six months ago, Crump had been partnered up with Gray, a 22-year, highly decorated officer with 20 years in the violent crimes division. Gray was also a best-selling author of three books on criminal profiling. Crump wanted to work with him because he heard all about the impressive busts Gray had made, including catching Marcus Foran, the notorious Gablewood Park Strangler; seven serial rapists; fifty-two murderers, and closing hundreds of other violent offender cases — all with an impressive conviction record that made Gray one of District Attorney Orson Helmer's favourite people.

Crump remembered being surprised when he was first introduced to Gray. He imagined he'd be balding, badly overweight, and have a drinking problem. He didn't expect to meet a man with a full head of raven black hair, broad shoulders, bulging biceps, and hands that look like they could punch through brick walls. No alcohol dependency, either. He thought one of Gray's most unique characteristics was that he didn't appear to have any self-destructive vices. It just seemed strange for a cop who had experienced everything he had on the job.

Gray had kept himself in peak physical condition most of his adult life. He was a Gold Knuckles boxing champ when he was in the academy. Back then he was known as "The Sandman" for his ability to put other boxers to sleep on the mat. That was another trait D.A. Helmer loved about Gray.

"Hey Sandman, ready to deliver the left cross of justice today?" Helmer asked as he walked by Gray and Crump, not acknowledging the rookie's presence.

Gray offered Helmer a nod and forced grin. Helmer nodded back, smiled, and continued walking. Helmer sent congratulatory cigars to Gray after every big conviction, a turkey every Thanksgiving Day, and a decorative ornament every Christmas. It all made Gray feel mildly uncomfortable. Gray always gave the cigars away to other officers eager to puff their lives away, and the turkeys and ornaments to the local rescue station. Gray thought gifts from the D.A.'s office were highly inappropriate — like digging through someone's desk without their permission.

Gray believed in rules and enjoyed enforcing them. He had a bit of a mean streak he liked to let out on lawbreakers that resisted arrest, but that wasn't the reason he became a detective. It was his passion for profiling and tracking down violent offenders that made him want to get up in the morning, and he was good at it. His ability to track and profile criminals made him highly sought after by various departments at his precinct.

Unlike most of his brothers in blue at Division 22, Gray was an academic before joining the academy. He received top honours and a master's degree in criminal psychology from the University of Waterloo for his thesis paper on the Gablewood Park Strangler more than 20 years ago. Gray's thesis paper focused on a building a psychological profile of the killer. It generated new leads for the police and ended up playing a vital role in his apprehension, something the TPD took notice of instantly. After joining the academy, the TPD fast-tracked Gray to detective in the violent crimes unit under now-retired Captain Phillipe Gaston, who was replaced by the competent, but less passionate, Captain Kramer Gleeb. The latter had little interest in Gray outside of his high conviction rate. That suited Gray just fine; he always hated being micromanaged.

"So, Detective Gray," Crump said as he walked over to the coffee machine to get his third cup of the day. "What scumbag are we hunting today?"

Gray pulled a brown file from one of his newly organized desk drawers and tossed it on Crump's desk.

"We're on a cold case until something fresh comes along. Henry Sift, a small-time thief, pulled a lot of jobs for local gangs. Forty-two years old and single. He was found dead in the alley behind Ricardo's Meat and Deli on Glacier Street more than a month ago. He took two slugs in the back of the head."

"Execution-style killing. Shouldn't this be with guns and gangs?" Crump asked.

"They were unsuccessful in generating any leads through their regular channels, but there's another angle the captain wants us to look into. Sift's privates were badly mutilated in the attack and it doesn't match any of the local gangs' MOs. The coroner said it happened shortly before he was killed. It could be an ex-lover, a professional killer trying to throw us off their scent, another random, mindless killing or something else."

"So what's our first step?"

"We've already taken it. We've got the coroner's report and photographs of Sift. Now we need to speak with his known accompl–"

"Drop that file, rookie," Captain Gleeb yelled from across the room.

Crump plopped the file down on his desk immediately.

"Get over here, Gray. We've got a hot one."

Gray jumped to his feet, grabbed his jacket, and made his way over to Captain Gleeb. Crump took a half-eaten doughnut out of his mouth, wiped his face semi-clean with his sleeve and followed his mentor.

"Here's a weird one for you," Gleeb said. "A middle-aged guy was killed at a used car dealership he works at in Old Toronto. His skull was caved in by an air conditioner in his office. I've got some uniforms there, controlling the scene as we speak."

"I guess someone didn't like their leasing options," Crump said, grinning at his superiors.

Gleeb chuckled, which expanded the grin on Crump's face until Gray's disapproving look wiped the rookie's smile clean off.

"Get your coat, Crump. We're going car shopping."

3

Memories of Yesteryear

As I drove to my apartment, possibly for the last time, I found myself lost in warm and wonderful memories I had experienced in my modest home. It was my place of refuge for many years. I will always remember the day I moved in as the day I met Rose.

The sun was shining, the rat-ravens were chirping and fluttering about the midday sky, and just in the distance you could see all the colours of the rainbow. It was the most beautiful rainbow I had ever seen. Shades of pink, orange and red filled the sky with an array of visual delights. It was nothing short of a miracle, provided by Mother Nature and years of lax industrial pollution laws.

I was twenty-four years old and saw Glamerica as a place where I could make my mark on the world. The country controlled the majority of the resources on the planet, so I couldn't think of a nation better-equipped to help me make something of myself, whatever that something might be. I had spent the last four years of my life travelling the globe in an attempt to find my calling. Unfortunately, every country I visited was

suffering from severe economic depression and debilitating ill-
nesses — largely due to famine, pollution, or a lack of internal
organs. My limited education reduced my chances of finding
any sort of decent employment, since the only job shortages
appeared to be in the medical field, so I decided to move back
to my hometown of Mississauga. I figured the worst-case scenario would be that I'd never find my calling, in which case I
would slack in style for the rest of my life. It didn't seem like a
bad option.

When I first arrived I had little money and no place to live,
so I decided to go to Just Caffeine, a small café in the Black
Light District of Old Bramptonia. I figured I could brainstorm
a way to find a new home and some cash over a cup — or six
— of coffee and half a pack of smokes. It was there I saw the
advertisement that would change my life forever. As I drank
the last sip of my third complimentary refill, a poster of one of
the nation's favourite tools of propaganda caught my eye. It was
Uncle Glam. His silver-haired, Adonis-like body was flexing his
exaggerated biceps atop a mound of rotted humanity in front of
several pristine condominium buildings. He held the freshly cut
liver of a harvestee in one hand and a pitchfork in the other. His
eyes, black as night, felt like they pierced into my soul. It was a
truly eye-catching poster. It read, "Glamerica wants you to have
this condo!"

I couldn't believe my eyes. After all the time I spent gal-
livanting around the world, my hometown had welcomed me
back with open arms. I dropped my cup and ran out the door
towards the Glamerican Ministry of Affordable Housing,
which was a mere five blocks away. I was so excited at the
thought of having a home of my own again that I didn't notice
I was being followed.

I ran, then jogged, then walked and gasped for air, for the
first four-and-a-half blocks before I was stopped by a large,
middle-aged woman with medium-length, dirty blonde hair,

an apron, and arms the size of an eight-hundred pound gorilla. Apparently, my dream of becoming a homeowner drowned out the angry screams of my pursuer for the past ten minutes.

"Hey deadbeat, you owe me for four cups of coffee and a new poster," the woman said in an angry tone.

It was the woman that worked the counter at Just Caffeine. I had forgotten to pay for my drinks — apparently the last three cups were not complimentary. I took this opportunity to brush off any rust I might have developed for charming an old-fashioned Glamerican woman during my travels. I was once known as quite the sweet talker.

"I am so sorry," I said, which is always a good way to start a conversation with an angry woman. "I completely forgot about the bill. Please accept my apology."

The anger lines in her face began to deteriorate — a good sign.

"Well," she replied. "I'll let it go this time, but you best not mess with ol' Bessie again. Now pay for your drinks and I'll forget all about it."

It looked like I still had the right stuff. All I had to do is finish the conversation with a flattering and witty remark.

"My dear Bessie, I would never purposely offend a woman of your size — err, I mean, it's just that your arms are so massive, you could probably pick me up by my skull and peel me like a banana. No, wait, this is coming out all wrong. Have you ever seen *King Kong*? It's a classic film where–"

The next thing I knew, Bessie, the ape-armed barista, had swatted me off my feet, picked me up over her head, and was spinning my fragile frame around in the air. Her technique would have been perfect for making pizzas.

"You're in the wrong profession," I yelled as I spun helplessly in her arms.

It didn't take long for me to feel ill. Motion sickness has always been a problem with me. I probably would have returned

Bessie's four cups of coffee to her if not for her Olympic-styled shot put toss of my body. I flew helplessly over a bus shelter as my liquid lunch rained down on half a dozen horrified pedestrians who were waiting for the Route 66 bus. I landed in the shrubs just outside the parking lot of the Glamerican Ministry of Affordable Housing.

I crawled out of the shrubs, dusted myself off, and took refuge in the lobby of the centre. I glanced at a nearby mirror to survey the damage. After picking a few twigs out of my hair, I checked my clothes for vomit. Fortunately, none of my semi-digested projectiles landed on my acid-washed blue jeans, brown t-shirt or green hoodie.

"Sweet, I can still make a good first impression," I whispered to myself. "Today is my day to shine."

With a swagger in my step, I strutted over to the receptionist and asked her if there were any condos available for a man that was well-travelled and smelt faintly of coffee vomit.

"Hippies, skids, and drifters are to report to Lab 781 for their relocation," the woman said in a derogatory tone.

She appeared to find me as appetizing as a two-day-old doughnut filled with three-day-old jelly. I quickly reminded myself I needed to take the high road and ignore her crass comment. I took a deep breath and responded in a calm, polite fashion.

"Well then, I'll go and introduce myself to the people in this fine organization that are of some sort of importance," I said.

At first the woman just rolled her eyes in response, but after I gave a small bow and humble greeting to the office's communal stapler and water cooler, she looked as if someone had just dropped their pants and defecated on her desk.

My work here was done.

As I strolled down the brightly lit corridor labelled "Happy Harvest Labs 781 – 871," I remembered all the poor souls halfway across the world who had been sacrificed so my fellow

Glamericans and I could continue our gluttonous way of life. I remember thinking it strange that with the organ scare long over there were still laboratories designed for harvesting procedures. Perhaps they were harvesting something else these days, like peaches. I love peaches. Maybe the signs simply hadn't been changed. My pondering came to an abrupt end as I spotted Lab 871. Phew! I almost missed it.

I knocked on the door three times and yelled, "Open, says-a-me!" It was one of my favourite lines from cartoons I watched as a child.

When the door opened, I was standing eye-to-eye with a beautiful young woman. She wore a white lab coat and a pair of protective yellow goggles. She removed the goggles and exposed her sparkling, emerald green eyes. Her hair was short and black, and her skin was pale and smooth, reminiscent of a porcelain doll. As she extended her hand to introduce herself, I was overwhelmed by her seducing scent, a mixture of vanilla and honey that made my brain feel happily hazy.

"Hey there, funny buns," the woman said. "I'm Rose. How can I help you?"

"I'm Remy. I'm interested in acquiring one of the condos in the posters you guys advertise."

Rose stared with disbelief. She grabbed me by the arm, pulled me inside her lab, and locked the door.

"Are you crazy?" she asked.

"Depends. Will that stop me from getting a free condo?"

"They're not exactly free. Where have you been?"

"Overseas."

"Well, that's probably a good thing. The Glamerican government created that program to reduce the number of homeless people in the Greater Toronto Area."

"Wow. And people say socialism is dying."

"It's the homeless that are dying."

"Even more reason to get them off the street and into a condo."

Rose stared at me with a look of pity and stroked my hair.

"Oh, Remy. The government has been tricking people into trading vital organs for free homes. After their organs are removed they quickly fall ill and pass away. Since most of the people that agree to the trade are homeless and long cut off from their families, and without legal wills, it's often difficult to notify a next of kin, so their condos get seized by the government and are redistributed to other willing harvestees. You really haven't heard about this?"

"Nope. Glad you let me in on the secret though, Rose. I need my organs."

"When the story broke last year it made front-page news around the world."

"I don't do a lot of reading."

"It was on every news channel across the globe."

"I don't own a television."

"Well, anyways, the program was downsized after the news broke. The government didn't really mind, since it had already reached its harvesting quota."

I was paralytic from the shock of hearing her horrid tale. It took me a few moments to regain my composure and continue the conversation.

"So, just out of curiosity, what do you harvest here?" I asked.

Rose gazed at me for a moment, her tender-looking lips forming an impish grin as she prepared to offer a response.

"Peaches," she said, holding out a fresh, fuzzy fruit. "Would you like one?"

I breathed a sigh of relief and happily accepted her offer of nature's nectar. After devouring the delicious fruit, I asked her if she knew of any available lodgings for a man strapped for cash. Rose grabbed my arm again, yanked me out of her lab and led me towards the building's back entrance.

"Hey Gloria, I'm taking my lunch break," she yelled as we exited the centre.

She continued to pull me by my arm until we reached her car in the company parking lot.

"I've been waiting for a new neighbour for almost two years," she explained. "My apartment feels so empty. I'd love to have a nice guy nearby to hang out with. My gut tells me you're sweet. I'm sure a little angel like you would never cause any trouble. So how about it, do you want to be neighbours?"

Rose stared at me, eagerly anticipating my response. Her eyes shined twice as bright as before. Her beauty dumbfounded me. Rose could have asked to borrow my head at that moment and I would have happily plucked it from my shoulders and placed it in her delicate hands. This woman formed a tighter grip around my heart with a twenty-minute chat and a smile than any other woman over my entire life. For the first time ever, Cupid had successfully struck me with an arrow of romantic bliss. Damn that dirty, diaper-wearing bastard.

"Of course I'll take the place," I said, not realizing how stupid it sounded to agree to rent an apartment I had never stepped foot inside. Rose appeared to enjoy my ability to make hasty, uninformed decisions.

"Great," she replied. "Let's go introduce you to your new home."

Rose whizzed through the inner-city streets of Mississauga, obviously extremely knowledgeable of the area. She turned onto Hazel Drive and followed a path filled with extensive brick-work until we arrived at a pair of mustard yellow buildings. She parked the car in front of Building A — Maple Leaf Towers. We exited the vehicle and headed towards the entrance to my new lair. The retina scan at the front door swiftly approved of Rose's lovely lashes and we were given entrance to the main lobby. I followed her to the superintendent's office, which wasn't hard to find. Old pieces of cardboard with the words "Super's Place" were written in black marker and duct taped along the walls. Each sign had an arrow pointing people in the right direction. I picked up the scent of several delightful aromas coming from the apartments we walked by. It was like walking through the world's kitchen and being allowed a tiny whiff of a seemingly infinite number of delicacies. Rose came to a halt at apartment twenty-two. She knocked gently on the door, stepped back, and took a beautiful and graceful stance. The door opened and revealed a bald, heavy-set white man standing in his undergarments, whose stomach protruded outwards a foot further than his chin. His wife-beater tank top was a shade of yellow I hadn't seen before. The man leaned against the entrance to his home and slid his right hand into his tighty-whities for a relieving scratch as he began to address us.

"Hey Rosie, what can the super-man do for you today?"

"Hi Cletus," she replied, accustomed to his half-dressed greetings. "I found someone that wants to rent the apartment beside mine. This is my friend, Remy."

Cletus looked at me and smiled a half-toothed grin — which would have been a toothy grin if he wasn't missing half his teeth.

"Well, hey there tiny, the name's Cletus. Glad to meet ya," he said as he made his way into the hallway, removed his hand from his stained, sweaty undergarment and extended it towards me. I returned his gesture of friendship with a hearty handshake, praying that Rose would invite me into her place afterwards for a delousing.

"So, you want to rent the place next to Rosie," Cletus said while scratching his scalp. "I guess that would be alright, just as long as you've got first and last. That'll be five thousand smack-a-roos."

I swallowed hard and tried to brainstorm a way to get Cletus to accept me with the five hundred dollars I had left to my name. He picked up on my discomfort immediately.

"What's the dilemma?" he asked. "You ain't got that much?"

Before I could respond Cletus continued to speak, as if he already knew I was suffering from a cash flow crisis.

"Well, I tell you what, you give me what you got on ya and you can work off the rest," he said. "I need somebody to de-clog all the drains on the fourth floor."

"Ouch!" Rose responded, obviously knowing something about the fourth floor I was not going to like. Oh well, it can't be worse than fighting a hobo for an alley in Copenhagen.

I handed my cash to Cletus and gave him a big smile.

"Cletus, you have yourself a tenant."

He let out a hearty laugh and slapped me on the back with his right hand, making me curse inside my head for being broke and having to burn my only shirt. He went back inside his apartment and returned a few minutes later with a set of old keys.

"Here are the keys to apartment seventy-one on the seventh floor," Cletus said. "Rose will show you where it is. You two have a good night and I'll see you bright and early tomorrow morning."

Cletus walked back into his home and slammed the door behind him. Rose looked at me and smiled.

"Welcome home, Remy," she said.

"Welcome home, indeed," I replied.

"Moo," she said.

Moo?

My reminiscing was cut short by a loud, metal crumpling smash-like sound. Apparently, while I was walking through memories of yesteryear, I had completely forgotten I was driving my new van. I had driven it right past my apartment complex, beyond the Mississauga city limits, straight through a small wooden fence and into a farmer's field. It was there my daydreaming came to an abrupt end, when my van collided with a cow. It was no ordinary cow, either. It was Daisy, Queen of the

Toronto Dairy Cows. I had seen her on various milk cartons over the years. Her owner forced her to wear a tiara because it made her easy to recognize. Unfortunately for her, she now looked more like a ninety-nine cent ground beef special than a prize-winning cow. The front of my van had been badly damaged and stained with the entrails of the unsuspecting heifer. Moments later, a farmer ran towards me, yelling profanities and gripping a shotgun. He looked upset.

"You killed Daisy, you bastard!" he yelled while firing off a round of buckshot into my windshield.

I ducked down, frantically gripped the gear shifter and tried to reverse the van. I slammed on the gas and shot forward. In my state of panic, I accidently put the van into drive, running over Daisy's skull and fatally colliding with the angry farmer. I felt a little guilty about killing the man, but I'm sure he didn't feel his life was worth living anymore now that his prized cow was gone. I probably did him a favour. Besides, the shotgun I looted from his mangled corpse was still in pretty good condition and could fetch a decent price at the Central Office for the Sale and Trade of Consumer Objects, or C.O.S.T.C.O. for short. I made my way back to the main road and headed towards my apartment. It was time to get this show on the road.

* * * *

Back at Tackyland Auto Sales, the office of the late Salvatore Santravera is being processed by detectives Gray and Crump. Crump is inspecting the body while the forensic photographer takes pictures. Gray is standing at Santravera's office door, observing the scene.

"Talk about a chilling killing," Crump said, provoking a snicker and grin out of the photographer.

"Focus on the scene, Crump," Gray replied. "Tell me what you see."

Crump took a couple of steps back from the body of Santravera and paused for a moment, waiting for the photographer to leave. He cleared his throat.

"Well, best I figure it, the victim thought he was making a sale and invited the killer into his office to close the deal."

"Go on," Gray said.

"Well, I figure the victim probably took a hit or two before the final blow with the air conditioner. The victim must have been incapacitated previous to the attack. I mean, look at him, he has no defensive wounds on his hands. No one just lets another person attack them with an air conditioner."

"You're partly right, Crump," Gray replied. "But look at the way the body is slumped in the chair. He appears to have been standing, leaning over the desk when the killing blow was delivered. For his attacker to hit him like this, he would have to hit him from behind."

Crump scratched his scalp in frustration, trying to understand the attack.

"But there's no room for another person to maneuver themselves properly behind the desk, let alone pick up an air conditioner over his head and smash it into the victim's skull with enough force to put his head through the bottom."

"Take a good look at the bottom of the machine, Crump."

Crump knelt down by the body and checked the bottom of the machine. While attempting to get back to his feet, he slipped in a small pool of oil and blood and stumbled backwards into one of the office walls, knocking down a small corkboard filled with sales reports. He quickly regained his composure and acted like it never happened. Gray rolled his eyes.

"It's plastic," Crump said.

"That's right, Crump. A lot of these older models were made with plastic bottoms to lower costs and market an easy-to-open maintenance door for repairs."

Crump nodded while trying to make sense of his mentor's words.

"Are you thinking the killer knew that? Do you think the killer has some sort of maintenance or HVAC background, and sabotaged the machine so it would fall at a particular moment?"

"Unlikely, but just to be safe find out if the dealership had scheduled any HVAC-related work to be done recently. It would be an easy way for our killer to come and go at their leisure," Gray responded. "There's a lot of oil at this scene. The victim has it all over his suit, and there's a trail that appears to lead to and from his office. It could be connected to how the killer got the drop on him."

Crump put the corkboard back on the wall and began to pick up the paperwork that had fallen on the floor. One note in particular caught the young detective's eye.

"Hey, Gray, what do you make of this?" he asked as he held up a piece of paper that stuck out amongst the reports. It was a napkin with I.O.U. written at the top in green crayon.

"Since when do car dealerships take an I.O.U. for a new car?" Crump asked with a puzzled look.

"They don't — especially when it's written in green crayon."

Gray removed a notepad and pen from his inner jacket pocket and began taking notes.

"Bag it along with every other piece of evidence in this office. I'm going to see where the oil trail ends."

Crump nodded and began bagging and boxing up various pieces of paper.

Gray followed the trail to the entrance of the used car lot. A uniformed officer who was questioning the other employees at the showroom entrance motioned to Gray to come over. The detective walked over to the officer, hoping there was a witness that saw something pertinent to the case, but Gray didn't hold his breath. He never had much faith in eye witnesses. He believed in hard evidence and eye witnesses didn't qualify.

He thought they were too unreliable. Hard evidence gets hard convictions, he always told his fellow officers. Speaking to the officer simply reinforced his belief.

"What do you have for me, officer?" Gray asked, trying to be patient with his fellow law enforcer.

"Not much, I'm afraid," the officer replied. "There was some sort of celebration going on. Almost the entire sales staff was wasted on tequila with the exception of your victim. All the other sales staff just received big bonuses for breaking the company's all-time sales record. Apparently your victim was the runt of the litter. He was left to man the car lot and showroom while the rest of them got all blotto."

"Interesting, the killer singled out the weak link," Gray said.

His last comment appeared to catch the attention of one of Santravera's co-workers, a man dressed in a pink and yellow blazer, white khakis and pink leather shoes. He wore yellow-framed eyeglasses and had a three-fingered ring on his right hand. It was shaped like a dollar sign.

"Weak ain't even the word, Holmes," said the loudly dressed man.

"Who are you?" Gray asked.

"The name is Carlos DeSantos, but the boys around here call me 'The Closer.'"

"Okay. Did you see anything suspicious, Mr. DeSantos?"

"I didn't see that chump Sal get whacked, if that's what you mean."

"Did you see anyone enter the showroom around the time of the attack?"

"Yeah, one guy walked onto the lot when I was going to take a leak. He was a little hard to see though, and to be honest I wasn't paying too much attention. Dude was tall, white, and scraggly looking. He was unshaven, had on a dirty, dark jacket. Man is lucky I didn't know what he was up to. No one comes around here and messes up my 'hood."

Gray looked up from his notepad for a moment and stared at Carlos. His right eyebrow arched in the manner it usually did whenever someone said something Gray thought was stupid. Carlos noticed his stare immediately.

"What, you don't think I could take that fool?" Carlos said in an annoyed, defensive tone, taking a step into Gray's personal space.

Gray liked his personal space.

"I didn't say anything, sir," Gray replied, taking a couple of steps back.

"You see this?" Carlos said, pointing at his left elbow.

"Your elbow?" Gray said as he tucked his pen and notepad back into his jacket pocket.

"Oh, this ain't my elbow," Carlos replied, while stepping towards Gray again. "This is the 'bow you don't want to know."

"Why are you talking like that?"

"Because it will knock your ass both to and fro," Carlos said, stepping even closer to Gray. He was now standing almost nose to nose with the detective.

"Please stop threatening me with rhyme, sir."

Carlos backed up half a step, and then began to make a gesture with his elbow. It was probably something crude, Gray thought, but just to be safe he grabbed the salesman's left arm, put it behind his back, and pressed his knee into Carlos' leg, forcing him down onto the showroom floor.

"Ow!" cried Carlos. "Man, what was that for? Let me go. I wasn't going to hit you, I swear."

"A wise decision, Mr. DeSantos," Gray said as he released the salesman. "Stick around in case any of the other officers have questions for you."

Carlos decided silence was the best policy this time around. He simply nodded to acknowledge Gray's request. The officer who had recently questioned the sales staff stood frozen, awaiting a response from the detective. Gray took his notepad back out and continued jotting down notes.

"Good work, officer. Make sure I get a copy of all the witness statements," Gray said as he continued to follow the oily trail.

"Sure, no problem, detective," the officer said as he motioned for another officer to check on Carlos.

As Gray walked out of the showroom, he noticed a shadowy figure inside a black sedan parked just outside the car lot. The man appeared to be snapping photos of the crime scene, probably a reporter looking to make a few quick bucks at the expense of the victim. Gray didn't care for reporters who cluttered his crime scenes, but he did respect their search for the truth. He decided to ignore the shutterbug and instead focused his attention on Crump, who was standing beside a large oil drum that was dripping oil all over the pavement. He didn't know if the rookie witnessed his recent altercation with DeSantos, nor did he care. Gray had little patience for people who didn't respect law enforcement officers and that went double for people who invaded his personal space.

"I think this is where the initial struggle took place, boss," Crump said. "This area is covered in oil. I'll have the forensic team check it out."

Gray nodded and started following another oily trail that led to an empty spot on the lot.

"This must be where he made his escape," Gray said while staring down at the end of the trail. "Crump, is the dealership missing any vehicles?"

"Yeah, a van. But here's the weird thing, it wasn't even ready to be sold yet. It hadn't even been painted. It was only on the lot because of renovations being performed at the Fraud plant down the street. Apparently, the plant needed extra space so nearby dealerships were holding on to a few unfinished vehicles. Also, there's an old sedan here that isn't part of their inventory."

"Interesting," Gray said as he processed his young partner's information. "If the killer came in on foot, taking the van could be nothing more than a convenient way to flee the scene. However, if he brought another vehicle with him, he may be trying to tell us something. Have the vehicle processed at the lab and grab the victim's paperwork. I want to go through it with a fine-tooth comb, starting with the I.O.U."

Crump nodded, pulled a small evidence bag out of his jacket that contained the crayon-covered napkin and handed it to Gray.

"What do you think all of this means, Gray?" Crump asked.

Gray held up the evidence bag and attempted to decipher the note.

"I don't know, Crump, but I think whoever killed this man wasn't just looking for a new van."

"What are you saying?"

"I'm saying if we don't find the killer fast, I think we'll be finding more bodies before this is over."

"A serial killer?"

"I'm not sure. But I get the feeling whatever this person is trying to accomplish, this is just the beginning. He doesn't care who gets in the way of his goal. This man brutally attacked a middle-aged salesman in broad daylight, and then stole a vehicle from the car lot, but not before leaving a note behind written in crayon. This isn't the work of a gun-for-hire or a car thief. This is something else. I don't think this location was selected by chance, either. The salesmen here appear to be a bunch of degenerates. There's no security staff or video, and he handpicked the weakest link on the food chain. I think he's trying to send us a message, and he's daring us to catch him."

"What do you think the message is?"

"Could be anything, Crump, I've seen it all. For all we know this guy has daddy issues and likes to take them out on anyone fitting the victim's description, or he could think he's the king of the unicorns and he's fighting off angry minotaurs trying to invade his kingdom. All we know right now is that he's dangerous and we need to stop him. Let's get back to the office and analyze the note. It's our best bet at figuring out where he'll strike next."

"Nothing more dangerous than a fool with a crayon and a cause."

"He's dangerous, Crump, but this one is no fool," Gray replied as he stared long and hard at the note.

* * * *

Later that night at the Toronto Supernova Gazette, journalist Monica Burke put the finishing touches on her front page article about the mysterious car lot killer.

"'The Car Lot Killer,' it's got a nice ring to it," Monica said to her editor, Johnson Nash, as she typed away on the trusty laptop she had been using since her days in j-school.

"You know what would make this story even better, Burke?" Johnson asked.

"What's that, boss?"

"If you used one of the company's computers instead of that relic of yours. It must make all your stories take twice as long to bang out."

"Meh, apples are apples."

"Tell that to the turn on page three, where the rest of your story needs to be in twenty minutes. I haven't even edited it yet."

"Don't worry, it's top-quality copy."

"This is coming from the same person who misspelled 'county' in the headline 'Mississauga's County Track Stars.'"

"Anyone can forget an 'o' once in a while," Monica said with a smile as she continued to type. "Besides, aren't you the editor that missed that one?"

"Yeah, and I have the scars on my ass from the proud track parents' boots to prove it. Just hustle with the copy so I can give it a onceover."

"Done. It's making its way to your inbox as we speak," Monica said as she kicked her feet up on her desk for a well-deserved rest. Her beige skirt slid up past her knees, exposing her long legs and brown cowboy boots. She untied her ponytail and leaned her head back, letting her medium-length, brown curly hair down for a moment, before placing her black cowboy hat over her face for a quick snooze. Monica always fancied herself a cowgirl. It stemmed from her roots out west in Alberta, where her father raised her on a ranch just outside the Greater Calgary Area, or the GCA as she referred to it. She looked out of place in Toronto, but she didn't care. Her charming personality and energy attracted people to her like moths to a flame — and much like moths to a flame, people often got burnt. Not because she enjoyed hurting people, but because people tended to tell her more than they should — especially men. That made her an invaluable asset to the newspaper giant that employed her.

Johnson smiled as he read her copy. It was the kind of quality reporting he had come to rely on Monica to produce.

"Great job, Burke. How did you get all these details about the murder? I thought the police were keeping a tight lid on it."

Monica's response was semi-muffled by the hat she left on her face.

"They are, but stupid boys talk to pretty girls."

"That's why I love you, Burke. You're more than happy to prostitute your smile for a story."

"Just as long as it's only the smile," Monica replied, lifting her hat off her face just enough to give her editor a wink.

Johnson let out a short laugh.

"Good job. Go get some rest and I'll see you in the morning."

"Sure thing, Johnson. Catch you later," Monica responded as she got up, grabbed her purse, and left the newsroom to go to her apartment.

* * * *

Gray arrived home at 8:30 p.m. He pulled all his notes from his jacket and laid them out on his kitchen table. He put on a pot of coffee and stood hovering over the notes, staring at them until his java was brewed. Gray always enjoyed building profiles on potential homicide suspects, particularly in situations where the crimes weren't cut and dried. The violent and bizarre death of Salvatore Santravera, the oil trails and the missing car told Gray that he was dealing with someone extremely impulsive that was likely prone to commit violent acts with little or no provocation. But then there was the I.O.U. written in crayon, as if done by a child. Once the hand writing was matched to a suspect it would be pretty damning evidence to help the district attorney place them at the scene. The perp even admitted to the petty theft. It was as if he was daring the police to try and catch him, as if the brutal murder of an innocent man was just a game. The safety meeting comment only fuelled that line of thinking in Gray's mind. That kind of arrogance irked him, while simultaneously sending a surge of adrenalin through his body. The challenge was reminiscent of the chase that led up to the capture of the Gablewood Park Strangler.

The strangler was a taxi driver that worked the night shift in downtown Toronto's financial district. He took the lives of eighteen women before he was finally apprehended with the help of a young, up-and-coming police officer. That officer was Tobias Gray. As much as his role in Foran's arrest helped jumpstart his career, Gray secretly hoped he would never again encounter such a monster. While his superiors and the media held him up as a role model for future law enforcement officers,

Gray considered the case a failure. He was recruited seven murders into Foran's killing streak and felt partially responsible for every life taken after that. Never again, he told himself as he looked over the notes in front of him. Gray grabbed a mug of black coffee and sipped it as he put together the initial profile of a new enemy of the people of Toronto.

Suspect: Unknown

Gender: Male

Description:
-Tall, Caucasian, "Scraggy-looking," unshaven
-Wearing dark jacket, possibly covered in oil

Behaviour:
-Prone to impulsive, violent acts
-May see crimes as a game (I.O.U left at scene)

Additional notes:
- Suspect may have mechanical background
- Driving stolen van (silver)

4

NOBODY LIKES THE FRENCH

After arriving at my apartment and loading the van with my worldly possessions, I headed towards my second destination. I burned the entire day obtaining transport and moving furniture, so the last thing I wanted to do was spend more time collecting supplies. Who knew how long I'd have to complete my quest? I hit the road at 9:12 p.m. on Thursday night. I drove along the eastbound Hwy. 401, racing through Cobourg, Belleville, Kingston, Brockville and Cornwall, praying to myself the entire drive that I would have enough time to complete my quest and make it back to Rose to enjoy our final minutes together.

I tensed up as I came upon a road sign for the New Quebec border: "New Quebec Border 'N' Rest Stop – 25 km."

As I headed towards the border, thoughts of the formation of Ontario's neighbour to the east filled my mind.

When the Americanadian Constitution on Rights and Freedoms was chiselled out — shortly before the merger — both nations agreed that French would be removed as a national language. This sparked outrage throughout the province of

Quebec, as well as parts of Atlantic Canada, especially within New Brunswick's Acadian population.

Both Quebec and New Brunswick held referendums to separate from Canada before the merger with the U.S. The result in Quebec was a long-awaited landslide victory for separatists, while the result in New Brunswick was much closer, resulting in a 55/45 split in favour of separation. Although the French population was significantly outnumbered in New Brunswick, many English-speaking residents wanted no part of a merger with the U.S., so New Quebec was born.

The American and Canadian federal governments allowed New Quebec to form and function as an independent nation, but there were several stipulations.

Many years before the merger, Quebec had built powerful hydro-electric power plants that produced a great deal of electricity for Canada and the United States. As time passed, more and more electricity was required to power the vastly expanding economies of both countries. By the time the two countries merged, Quebec's plants were powering twenty per cent of Americanadian cities. In exchange for New Quebec's sovereignty, its government agreed to supply Americanadian cities with power at no cost. The Government of New Quebec also agreed to give Americanada a steady supply of lumber — so they could rebuild the old Canadian battleships and commando canoes. The deal would have bankrupted the newly formed fledgling nation if not for the soaring cost of maple syrup per barrel.

The majority of New Quebecers wanted nothing to do with Americanada, but knew an alliance would be essential for their survival. In return, the two countries' borders would remain open for free trade. Since Glomitrox knew how miniscule a security risk New Quebec posed when it took over, the countries' borders had remained open and unguarded to this day.

I continued to drive my van towards my next destination until about 2 a.m. on Friday, when the off ramp for the Glamerica–New Quebec border rest stop became clear.

Thank the Gods, I've had to sprinkle a tinkle since Mississauga!

* * * *

"I don't know, Toby, the 'Car Lot Killer' doesn't sit well with me," Crump said as he scrolled through the Friday morning digital edition of the Gazette at 6 a.m., while enjoying his fourth doughnut. "I would have preferred something like, 'Ice-cold killer leaves salesman with a head condition-er.'"

"Personally, I would have preferred that people keep quiet and stop leaking details about the crime scene to the press," Gray replied, obviously annoyed with his young partner's attempt at humour. "By the way, call me Toby again and those doughnuts won't be the only things in this office with a hole through them."

"Sorry, detective," Crump said with his mouth half full.

"So what's the motive here, Crump? It was obviously not just a simple robbery. The killer wanted us to find that note. There might be a clue in here as to where the killer will go next," Gray said as he rummaged through the box of evidence collected from the crime scene.

"Not sure yet, sir. The van hasn't been spotted within city limits by our boys, so the killer may have fled the area. The car lot's neighbourhood is a dump and the traffic cams in the area haven't worked for years, so we haven't been able to get a decent mug shot yet. And the dealership hasn't scheduled any HVAC-related work to be done in months, so that's looking like a dead end as well."

"Be patient, Crump. That van should stick out like a sore thumb. The killer will surface soon, but for now we need to stay focused on the message. The perp made a point to leave oil all over the scene, as well as a note written in green crayon."

"Irradiated emerald crayon, according to our lab boys," Crump replied.

"Interesting. You think it's a clue, Crump?"

"I think anything could be a clue right now."

"Good. That's the way a detective should think."

Gray and Crump's discussion was interrupted by their Captain, as he approached the desks of the two detectives.

"Gray, do you have any suspects yet for the car lot killing?" Gleeb asked.

"Not yet, Captain, but the van will have to surface soon. Right now we're going over the clues, trying to determine the killer's motive and where he'll likely be next."

"Well, I have some good news and some bad news for you," Gleeb replied. "The good news is the van was spotted about 15 miles outside of the Toronto area at a small dairy farm."

"What's the bad news?" asked Crump.

"It was found fleeing the scene of a grizzly hit-and-run with at least one dead," Gleeb replied. "I told our people that nobody touches anything until forensics arrives on the scene." Gray's eyes lit up as he jumped from his chair and hastily made his way out of the building. Crump grabbed the address of the farm from Gleeb and sprinted out of the office to catch up to his mentor.

"I'm right behind you, Gray. Let's go catch ourselves a killer."

* * * *

I parked my van and sprang out in a panic. I looked around for a restroom that could end my "pee-mergency." My bladder's salvation was about 50 feet away, attached to a small, dirty building that resembled a port-o-potty on steroids. I didn't think I would make it, so I gripped my best friend and poor decision maker tightly and began an awkward run to the bathroom. My movements attracted the attention of an elderly man who was barbecuing hotdogs outside of his RV a few parking spots away from my van. As I passed him all I could hear was his girlish giggle. "Looks like someone's got a case of the squiggly-wigglies," he said as he laughed at my discomfort.

That old troublemaker was lucky I had much more important matters to attend to. I tore open the door to the musty bathroom and shuffled my way to the mustard-stained urinal in front of me. Within a flash, my pants were unbuttoned and bundled around my ankles as I cried out a sigh of relief. "Oh yeah, that's what daddy likes!"

Damn! If only I realized the cost of such hasty pants-tossing sooner. I gazed down at my feet midstream and watched as my pants absorbed a puddle of urine donated to the restroom floor by a recent passerby. Although I was relieved to have my bladder back to its normal size, it felt like little consolation to having someone else's pee on my pants. I carefully slipped them off, picked them up, and began walking back to my van in my lime green briefs to find a replacement pair.

My pants dripped a foul-smelling yellow trail on my way back. I stopped for a moment to observe four hotdogs on a barbecue that had been left to sizzle, unattended by the elderly owner of the RV. I picked up a bun, placed one of the wieners inside and gobbled it down while tracking the movements of the old smart ass. He was in the rest area's convenience store, probably purchasing condiments for his snack. Silly old man, you should have come to me first. I can spice up these dogs for you. Deciding the short-term pain was worth the long-term gain, I clenched my pants in both hands, lifted them over the unsuspecting grill and its all-beef inhabitants and twisted. The crackling sounds on the grill filled the air with an acidic aroma, leaving me feeling a little better. I tossed the pants into a nearby trash bin, grabbed a pair of old jeans from the back of the van, hopped inside, and drove away.

As I drove past the old man walking back to his meal, I stuck my head out of the driver-side window and cried out, "Next time watch who you smack with the wigglies, grandpa!"

The old man looked confused and offended. Now I felt much better. In retrospect, I probably did him a favour. Those wieners are packed full of fat and cholesterol.

Hot-doggity damn, I love helping old people!

* * * *

Gray and Crump drove up to the dairy farm's property line at 6:45 a.m. and parked just outside the line of yellow tape that ran across a section of fencing that was recently destroyed. Crump gave the top of his head a quick scratch and his eyes a rub as he walked around the splinters of wood and broken boards where the killer made his entrance and escape. The young detective had not yet given up his night life, so it usually took him a few hours to shake all the cobwebs loose during early morning calls.

"Looks like our guy busted in here in a hurry," said Crump, as the two detectives flashed their badges at the local law enforcement and walked inside the crime scene.

"Or out in a hurry," replied Gray.

Gray squatted by two clear sets of tire tracks that started in a section of muddy field near the broken fence and ended about 50 feet from the farmhouse. He spotted a group of forensic officers hovering around the other end of the tracks, and slowly moved towards them on a section of the tracks to avoid unnecessarily muddying his suit. Crump walked over to his side, stepping clumsily into a pile of mud that splashed the side of Gray's pants. Gray took a moment to leer at his partner.

"Oops. Sorry, boss," Crump said.

Gray pulled a pencil from the inside pocket of his jacket. He tapped it against his chin a few times before removing a notepad from the same pocket. Crump followed suit, standing ready to take notes about anything Gray might suggest about the crime scene.

Crump looked up and down the tracks twice.

"The tracks heading towards the fence don't show any pattern of acceleration," Gray said. "They're one smooth motion all the way to the end, as if the perp was just going for a relaxing drive in the country."

"What? You saying the perp didn't care about running through the fence and turning some farmer into ground round?" Crump asked.

"Not sure yet, it's strange, though. The tracks leaving the property look more erratic. The pattern suggests someone in a state of panic."

Gray and Crump continued to follow the tracks until they came upon the first group of forensic officers, working the body of a dead cow.

"Howdy, boys. Got milk?" Crump said, getting a snicker out of forensic tech Juan Diaz, who was busy inspecting the remains. Diaz had worked crime scenes for 16 years, so he had seen his share of ugly shit. His warped sense of humour always helped him process the grizzliest of scenes.

"Why, Crump? You thirsty? Hey, Gray, can't they give you a partner that's a little older, like one that isn't still breastfeeding?" Diaz said, getting a rare smirk out of Gray.

"It's not my fault, Diaz." Crump said. "I kicked the habit twenty years ago, but your wife has got me back on it."

"Well, she does do a body good — look at these pipes," Diaz said as he flexed his oversized biceps and shared a laugh with Crump. Diaz kept things light at the crime scenes, a character-istic of Crump that always annoyed Gray. But Gray was never bothered by Diaz's antics. The fact that Diaz liked to pick on Crump was also a bonus to Gray, he liked watching them trade barbs, not that he would ever admit it.

"Anything interesting for us in that mess, Diaz?" Gray asked.

"More than you would expect from a dead cow," he replied.

"Allow me the honour of introducing Daisy, Queen of the Toronto Dairy Cows."

"Are you shitting me?" asked Crump.

"I am not my young, foul-mouthed friend," Diaz said as he lifted an evidence bag to Crump's face. It was a plastic bag filled with a bloody, mangled piece of jewelry.

"This is Daisy's tiara. Every year the prize-winning dairy cow is awarded one of these. It's platinum with diamonds and emeralds from what I'm told. Worth about ten grand. I'm surprised your killer didn't take it with him."

"I don't think our perp is after money, Diaz," Gray said. "Make sure that ends up on my desk as soon as you're done processing it."

"Sure thing. Don't sweat it. You'll be the first person I call," the forensic tech replied.

"Ya, Gray. Don't have a cow, man," Crump said.

"That's Detective Gray, rookie," Gray replied. "Anything else, Diaz?"

"Maybe. Your perp ran over the cow's skull, crushing it after it was already dead. That's why the tiara is so beat up. Also, the tire treads in the mud match a larger vehicle — like a van. Didn't your killer from yesterday steal a van?" Diaz asked. Gray nodded, saying nothing. He then began walking towards the second group of forensic officers. Diaz turned to Crump, who shrugged his shoulders.

"What can I say, Diaz? Gray has a way with people," Crump said. "Catch you later, milkman."

"Yeah, catch you later, doughnut sucker," Diaz replied as he went back to processing the scene.

Crump quickly caught up to Gray, who was standing over the broken body of the human victim. The less cordial Cassandra Crawford was the lead forensic officer working the scene. Crump tried to work his charm on her a few weeks before at a stabbing in Sherbourne Alley. He wanted her to rush the blood work on the victim and she told him where to go. It wasn't until a request came in from Gray that the case was given high priority. She and Gray met early into both of their careers, when Gray worked the streets and Crawford was a junior tech working for the city's chief coroner. They shared the odd smile at crime scenes, but the flirting appeared to stop at that. Crump figured Gray never slipped it to her since the two of them still seemed so friendly. Crump was a firm believer that once you've slept with a woman any relationship you've built up just goes downhill from there.

"This guy's neck was snapped," Crawford said to Gray, ignoring the presence of the young rookie detective. "Most likely from the impact of the van hitting him."

"Howdy, Cassie," Crump said, while smiling and winking.

"Hey, Crump," Crawford replied.

"So who's our lucky stiff?" Crump asked.

"Jonathan Redding, sixty-one years old, a member of the Glamerican Dairy Farmers' Association. Single. Lives alone. That's all we know about the victim so far," she said.

"That's more than we had," Gray replied, evoking a smile from Crawford. "Do you have a time of death?"

"Less than 24 hours ago," she replied.

"Two kills in one day," Gray replied. "This is not good."

"There's something else, Gray," she said. "The victim's hands are covered in gunshot residue, and we discovered a shotgun casing and pieces of glass near the body."

"The old geezer fought back," Crump said. "Do you know if the perp was hit?"

"Not yet. Between the cow and Redding there's a lot of blood to process here."

"Did you find the gun?" Gray asked. Crawford's smile turned to a look of concern.

"No, Gray. It looks like your killer took it with him. The good news is there's a set of footprints in the mud near the body. Size ten. Looks like sneakers. I'll let you know as soon as I have more."

"Thanks, Cassie," Gray said as he and Crump walked back towards the broken fence.

"Shit, this guy is armed now. As if he wasn't dangerous enough before," Crump said.

"I don't like where this is going, Crump," Gray said. "This attack is a very violent act and very public, much like the previous murder. We may be dealing with a serial killer."

Crump tried not to let his excitement show. The thought of working a big serial case with his mentor made his body pump with adrenalin.

"We'll catch this bastard, boss. He doesn't stand a chance," Crump said.

"Clear your head of that cocky bullshit, Crump. I need you focused."

"Sure thing, boss."

Gray stopped at the fence and spoke with the first officer on the scene. The officer said they were unable to find any witnesses to the crime, so far. A neighbour bringing the victim breakfast had called it in. Gray nodded, acknowledging the officer's work, and then headed towards his squad car with Crump. Before opening his door, Gray tried to brush some of the mud from his pants to no avail.

"I never thought of you as a dirty cop, Gray," a familiar voice said. Gray turned around and saw reporter Monica Burke standing behind him with a recorder and notepad in her hands. A camera was flung over one of her delicate shoulders. She was wearing tight blue jeans tucked into her brown cowboy boots and a white blouse. Crump winked at her, then hopped into the passenger side of Gray's car and waited for Gray to respond.

"So what's the deal here, Gray? I hear it's a hit and run, but I don't buy it. Not if you're here. You're the hunter of the hunters. What's going on?"

"People talk too much," Gray said, as he attempted to get into his car.

Burke leaned up against the car and gave Gray a big smile. Her blouse was partially unbuttoned, exposing her generous cleavage. "C'mon Gray, throw me a bone here. Or how about the Car Lot Killer — any leads? Are these crimes related?"

"No comment. Now go find some doe-eyed rookie working the beat if you want a quote, Monica. I've got a job to do," Gray said.

"C'mon, Gray, two murders in two days — this is front-page material."

"Goodbye, Ms. Burke. If you want a comment from the division, I suggest you call media affairs."

"Dammit, Gray, this feels like something big."

"I'll give you something big, sweetheart," Crump said, hanging his head out Gray's driver-side window.

"Crump, get your ass off my seat before you muck it up," Gray said.

Crump slid back inside the car, onto his seat.

"Fine, don't comment. I guess I'll have to do your job for you and find the connection myself," Burke said as she began walking towards the officers by the broken fence. Gray opened his car door and got inside. As he began the drive back to Division 22, he noticed a man in a baby blue suit sitting in a black sedan snapping photos of the crime scene from about 20 feet away. It looked like the car of the photographer from the scene of the Car Lot Killer.

"Crump, write down the license plate of that black sedan. I think it may have been at the used car lot. He's probably just another hack reporter looking to sell photos for a few bucks, but we should grab it just in case." Crump quickly scribbled down the license plate as they drove past the sedan: *K4A12L5.*

5
―――

A MISSION OF ACQUISITION

As I drove through New Quebec, I watched in amazement as the Glamerican midnight skies gave way to a beautiful chestnut-tangerine sunrise. The air filled my lungs with the tasty scent of maple. Advances in technology allowed maple farmers the ability to harvest sap year-round, which meant one could enjoy the sweet smell of maple on a hot, humid day in summertime or a snow-filled, chilly day in winter. As I drove by one of the maple farms, I decided to pull over and sample some of the sap.

I parked my van by a mound of dirt and leaves sitting on the side of the road. A member of the maple farm's security patrol was about 150 feet away, inspecting the grounds. I decided the best way to obtain a free sample without alerting the guard's attention was to blend in with my surroundings. There was a large puddle of mud a few feet into the northern lot of the maple farm. Carefully moving from tree to tree, I made my way to the puddle. I quietly slipped into the puddle and covered myself from head to toe. The mud was hot from the midday sun, and smelled like it may have been a bathroom for some of the local wildlife. Remembering the prize at stake, I forced down my body's desire to vomit and headed to the pile of leaves beside my van. I grabbed leaves by the handful and stuck them to my mud-covered body. After a few minutes of leaf labour, I was transformed into a heap of nature's droppings. It felt like I was back in kindergarten, gleefully creating a useless, messy tub of crap that the teacher would refer to as "art." I felt the desire to slap a happy face sticker with the words "Well Done!" on my ass. But not yet — my masquerade had only just begun.

I spotted the same security guard — or 'sapper' as they are known out in these parts — checking a tree's sap levels about 100 feet away. I darted from tree to tree, narrowly avoiding the sapper's line of sight. Every maple tree I attempted to siphon had already been harvested or wasn't ready to drip. The weathered metal pails screwed into the trees were empty. Frustrated, I kicked one of the buckets. The noise attracted the nearby sapper. I dropped to the ground in an attempt to disguise myself, but it was too late. The sapper grabbed the whistle tied to his neck and blew. A thin layer of sweat crept over my body as I began to panic; I knew what followed the sound of a sapper's whistle. I got up and ran towards my van. By the time I got to the driver-side door I could feel the ground tremble around me. It was getting closer. I leapt into the van, turned the key and slammed on the gas. The tires squealed as I narrowly avoided getting T-boned by a grizzly moose — half grizzly bear, half moose, all evil. The beast charged after me. I should have been able to speed away from the monster, but the van was having trouble accelerating due to my recent accident and the weight of all the furniture in the back. The beast rammed its antlers into the back of my vehicle. The sound of metal crumpling echoed throughout the van. I held the wheel tight and concentrated on keeping the van on the road. The creature rammed the van again, this time ripping the right-side backdoor completely off its hinges. Out of panic, I grabbed the shotgun from the passenger seat and fired blindly over my right shoulder. The kick from the shotgun slammed my right arm into the dashboard. I lost my grip on the gun and watched as the result of my blind firing unfolded. As the shotgun came loose from my grip, the left-side backdoor flew open and several pieces of furniture fell out of the gaping hole, along with my new-found weapon. The monster felt the fury of my bookshelf, night table and heavy wooden desk as they crashed onto the road. The furniture seemed to stop the creature dead in its tracks, allowing me to escape. I drove with my foot to the floor for two hours before stopping at an abandoned gas station to survey the damage. My rolly-chair, pull-out couch, grandma's rocking chair and a lamp shaped like a football were the only items that remained in the van. I turned the vehicle off, walked into the back and flopped onto my couch for a nap. Next time I think I'll just pay for the sample, I told myself as I drifted off into dreamland.

* * * *

After leaving the crime scene, Gray returned to Division 22 to finish up his day working on incident reports from the two murder scenes and to collect his notes. When he finished, he got into his car and headed towards home. The sun came down as he drove across the city, racking his brain for connections between the two victims. Cassie had left a phone message for Gray by the time he returned home. The glass left at the scene of the hit-and-run was the same type factory-installed on the van taken from Tackyland Auto Sales. This came as no surprise to Gray. He was already convinced the two crimes were connected.

Cassie also confirmed that the shoe prints in the mud belonged to a size ten sneaker, and the victim's feet were size twelve. He hung up his jacket in a closet by the front door, placed his holstered pistol on a closet shelf and made his way to the kitchen. Gray liked to turn his mind off for an hour and recharge after a long day. A hot meal and a stiff drink while solving the daily crossword in the Gazette was a welcome break to clear his mind before diving back into his case notes. Gray opened his fridge and looked around for something to eat.

"Shit," he mumbled to himself as he dug around in his pants pockets. He pulled out a crumpled grocery list from the day before. Gray walked out of the kitchen, grabbed his coat and exited the condo.

It was less humid than usual for a night in July, so he decided to walk to the 24-hour grocery store down the street. As he left the lobby of his building, he noticed a dark-coloured sedan parked on the opposite side of the street. He could see the shadowy outline of a figure behind the wheel. The car was parked next to a sign that read "No Parking Anytime, Violators Will Be Towed." Gray thought about walking over and informing the driver of the sign, but decided filling his belly was more important than preventing some high-priced lawyer from getting a ticket or a tow. The majority of the occupants in Gray's building were well-to-do businessmen and lawyers. He didn't particularly enjoy being surrounded by people who snubbed their noses at anyone in a blue collar, but the building was quiet, clean and the neighbours minded their own business. The combination made it easy for Gray to unwind after work and look over case files late at night without being disturbed. The condominium was more than most cops could afford, but Gray's royalties from the moderate success of his books more than made up for his salary's shortcomings. As he walked down Rogers Boulevard, Gray tried to remember cases he worked that were similar to the Car Lot Killer. He wasn't sure how to profile this killer just yet, but decided he would treat the suspect as a random serial until he could obtain more info. When Gray arrived at the small, all-night grocery store he picked up a plastic basket and pulled out his list: *Bread, Milk, Eggs, Chicken, Potatoes, Peanut butter.* He began collecting his groceries. Gray had only grabbed the bread and peanut butter when he spotted a dark-coloured sedan parked across from the store. This time the car was parked under a street light. It looked like the same car he saw at both crime scenes. Gray walked over to the cashier near the front of the store and placed his basket down on the counter. The bored-looking teen began to ring in Gray's purchase as the detective watched the driver of the sedan from a mirror in the store. The driver had slid onto the passenger seat and was snapping photos of Gray. He was wearing a black ball cap and his face was concealed behind a black hooded sweatshirt.

"That will be $12.64, sir," the clerk said without any attempt to be cheerful.

"Where are your eggs?" Gray replied.

"End of aisle six, in the coolers," the clerk replied while pointing to the back of the store.

Gray nodded and made his way down aisle six. After all his late-night grocery runs, Gray knew the store back to front. He knew the eggs were at the back of the store where he would be well-concealed from the shadowy shutterbug in the sedan. When he got to the end of the aisle, he pulled out his phone and called Crump. It took five rings for the young detective to answer.

"Hey, Gray, what's up?" the young detective asked. Gray could hear music from the Maritimes in the background. Crump was obviously looking over the case at his favourite watering hole.

"Detective Gray, rookie," Gray said. "Do you have any info on that sedan I asked you to check out earlier?"

"Not yet. I'm not sure why it's taking so long to get a plate I.D., but I have the plate number if that helps."

"Sure, fire it over to me."

"Okay. One second, boss."

Gray could picture his partner fumbling through the pockets of his beige trench coat, as he often did when looking for his notepad.

"The license plate is *K4A12L5*, Washington. Why do you want it now? Everything alright, boss?"

"I'll let you know. Keep your phone close by."

"You got it, boss."

Gray hung up the phone, picked up a carton of eggs and slipped out the shipping doors at the back of the store. He ran around the side of the building and up an alleyway. Gray ducked behind a parked car and sprinted across the street to a car parked about 20 feet away from the black sedan. He kept low to the ground as he crept up on the driver of the sedan. The license plate matched Crump's notes. Gray opened the carton of eggs, placed an egg in his left hand and lobbed it into the car through the driver-side window. It made a "splat" sound, followed by a string of curse words from the driver.

"Lousy, little punk bastards!" the man in the car yelled as he slid back onto the driver's seat.

The man stuck his head out of the driver-side window to continue cursing out whoever tagged him in the back of the head with an egg. Gray struck the left side of the man's face with a right hook. The impact from the punch knocked the right side of the man's forehead into the driver-side mirror, shattering it. Gray grabbed the stunned driver by the hood of his sweater and dragged him out of the car through the window. The man landed onto the sidewalk with a hard thud. He held the lacerated part of his forehead with one hand while reaching into his jacket with the other. Gray pulled Betty from his ankle holster and rested the barrel of his trusty snubnose revolver in between the eyes of the man, who froze immediately. Gray got his first good look at the man behind the camera. The man was white, middle-aged and slightly overweight. He was unshaven and smelled like he hadn't showered in a few days.

"Take your hand out of your jacket, nice and slow," Gray said as he watched the man's movements.

"Don't shoot, you goddamn psychopath," the man said. "I'm on your side."

"Yeah, my bad side. Now explain yourself before I have Betty here kiss you good night," Gray replied as he pulled the hammer back on his revolver.

"Jesus, Gray, what the hell is the matter with you? I'm F.B.I., Special Agent Ted Spacek."

Gray stared at him for a moment before responding.

"May I see some identification, officer?" Gray said while continuing to hold the revolver against the man's forehead.

Spacek slowly removed his I.D. and handed it to Gray, who inspected it while carefully removing his gun from the man's forehead. Gray slipped Betty back into his ankle holster, pulled Spacek to his feet and pushed him up against his sedan.

"Why the hell are you following me?"

"Orders from my superiors. They wanted to see what kind of leads you were creating in your homicide case at the car dealership," Spacek replied as he pulled a handkerchief from his jacket and held it against his bloody forehead.

"How's that the Feeb's business?"

"That's above your pay grade, detective."

"Oh yeah? Well next time call first and you might not end up with egg on your face."

"Fuck you, Gray. You'll be hearing from my superiors about this. You can't assault an agent of the F.B.I. Your captain is going to hear all about this in the morning."

"Then I'll make sure to be there bright and early."

Spacek got back into his car, slammed the door and sped off. Gray turned around to walk back to his condo and saw the store clerk standing about 10 feet away, holding a plastic shopping bag with peanut butter and bread. He was frozen in fear. Gray had no idea how long the kid had been standing there.

"Don't worry, kid. I'm a cop," Gray said as he flashed the clerk his badge.

The clerk nodded nervously before clearing his throat.

"I'm going to have to charge you for the eggs, sir," the clerk said.

Gray chuckled as he took twenty dollars out of his pocket and told the kid to keep the change. The clerk nodded, put down the shopping bag and ran back into the store.

Gray picked up his groceries and began walking back towards his condo.

* * * *

After flirting with the young, doe-eyed rookies working the scene of the Redding murder, Monica Burke spent most of her Friday night doing online searches from her desk at the Gazette office, trying to find a connection between the car lot killing and the hit-and-run at the dairy farm. The two victims didn't appear to have any connection to each other. Neither one had a criminal record. They didn't attend the same schools. They didn't run in the same social circles or associations. The victims lived two very separate lives. Online searches for Santravera were a bust as well. The most damning evidence Monica found on the car lot victim was online at RateMyDealership.com, where Tackyland Auto Sales was given several poor ratings for customer service and Santravera was called a crook by anonymous users. The search on Redding was a little more interesting, but didn't add much to her story other than a little background info on the victim. Redding had been interviewed in local newspapers and agricultural publications about the dairy market and he had posed with Daisy for pictures at various county fairs, where the cow showed off its fancy tiara. Monica already knew theft wasn't the motivation behind the attack. She had used her inviting smile, gift of gab and generously unbuttoned blouse earlier in the day to convince one of the younger, inexperienced officers at the crime scene to leak the details about the cow's tiara and the TPD's suspicion that these two recent killings were connected. Monica had enough information for her story in tomorrow's paper and even came up with her headline: "Oops-a-Daisy! Prized cow and owner found dead after hit-and-run. Another victim of the Car Lot Killer?" But the lack of motive behind the two killings left a bad taste in her mouth. What was the killer's motivation? Why had the police been unsuccessful in locating witnesses to identify the killer?

"Burning the midnight oil as usual, Burke," said Johnson as he lumbered out of his office, putting on his brown leather trench coat.

"The cops haven't been able to get a decent physical description of the killer yet," she replied.

"Not your problem, kiddo. Go home and get some sleep. That might be our front page story for tomorrow, but we've still got the rest of this week's papers to fill. You know you've got a county fair, a bake sale photo-op, sports profile and city council tomorrow."

"I know, boss; just trying to get inside the killer's head."

"Leave that part for the cops. And if they screw the pooch on the investigation, we'll make sure the public knows about it. That's how we serve and protect."

Monica shut down her computer, put on her coat and slung her laptop bag over her shoulder. She decided her editor was right this time around. Working the Car Lot Killer case was exciting, but exhausting, and the twelve other stories she needed for this week's newspapers weren't going to write themselves.

"Okay, boss, you win. I'm going to head home and crash for a few hours. I'll see you in the morning."

"Sounds good, Burke. I'll lock up here. Have a good night, kid."

Monica left the office, got in her beat-up red hatchback and started her drive home. The car sounded like an injured animal as she turned the ignition, and it winced as she planted the gas pedal to the floor when she got on the highway. She thought about getting another car from time to time, but her choice of careers made financing anything that wasn't absolutely necessary extremely challenging. Monica loved being a journalist more than anything in the world, but the pay stunk and it wasn't going to get any better. Very few daily newspapers still existed. The odd one, like the Toronto Supernova Gazette, was able to survive because it was the lead flyer distributor for companies in the Greater Toronto Area. Although the paper had decent online revenues, they didn't compare to what the flyer business brought in. Even though eighty per cent of the news read in the Toronto Area was done online, people still loved to flip through flyers to look for the latest deals, and once in a while they would even browse the print edition of the paper. Monica figured the elderly, crossword fans and coupon cutters comprised ninety-nine per cent of the newspaper's print readership, give or take a percentage point. Print or digital, Monica didn't care how the public got its news, just as long as it was reading. Worrying about revenues was beyond her pay grade and she liked it that way. All that interested her was educating the public and finding the truth, no matter how ugly. She thought about the car lot killing while driving, trying to guess where the killer might strike next. When Monica got off the highway, she pulled into a drive-thru coffee shop and pulled out a manila file that contained the photos she took at the two crime scenes. The Gazette's higher-ups frowned upon costly practices like printing out photos, which were deemed archaic and completely unnecessary many years before Monica became a journalist, but it helped her make sense of complicated stories, and since she was the newspaper's best investigative journalist, Johnson indulged her. She was only able to flip through a handful of images before she got to the drive-thru window and had to dig through her purse for change to pay for her coffee. The rest of the way home Monica's thoughts turned from her front-page story to a hot bath and a warm bed. Her apartment was a small, one-bedroom above a variety store on the east end of the city. After parking her car behind the store, Monica slung her purse and laptop bag over her shoulder and hastily stuffed her crime scene photos back into the manila file. She had to hold onto them with both hands to keep them from spilling all over the pavement. Monica bent over and picked up her coffee from her car's drink tray by biting down on the top of the paper cup and its plastic lid. She clumsily hip-checked the car door closed and made her way up the stairs on the side of the building towards her apartment. When she got to her front door, she fought with the old bolt lock, trying to get her key inside and jiggle it just right. After a few seconds, she heard a click and the door swung open. Monica tripped on a pair of dirty sneakers she had used to jog the morning before, spilling the contents of the manila file onto the old wooden floorboards that made up her hallway. The coffee she held between her teeth splashed up out of the lid when she stumbled and a small amount went up her nose. The coffee fell to the floor as she gagged for air and tried to blow the coffee out of her nostrils. She cursed her sneakers up and down as she used her jacket sleeve to save her photos from the coffee seeping onto them. Monica collected all the photos, cleaned them up as best she could and laid them out on her kitchen table to dry. After cleaning up her mess, she took a hot bath, changed into a pair of blue cotton pajama pants and a pink oversized t-shirt, then made her way into the kitchen to brew a hot tea and check on her photos. Knowing full well the kind of grief Johnson would give her for spending company dollars on prints just to ruin them the same day, she prayed they were still in good condition. After putting on the kettle, Monica sat down and began surveying the damage. A couple of the pictures were ruined, but most of them were fine. She breathed a sigh of relief for a moment, but then perked up when she noticed a man sitting in a black sedan with Washington license plates at both crime scenes. She got up from the table, poured some hot water into a mug and placed a camomile tea bag inside. Dipping the bag in and out of the hot water, she stared at the photos.

"Fuck the bake sale," she said to herself as she tossed the tea bag into the sink. Monica grabbed a jar of instant coffee from the cupboard and poured it into her tea as she fired up her laptop.

"Alright mystery man, let's find out who you are."

* * * *

When he returned home to his condo, Gray sat down on his couch and closed his eyes for a moment. He wanted to pass on looking over the case notes for one night. He knew a good night's sleep would do him well since tomorrow would likely be a long day, but couldn't shake the thought of a second Foran on the loose. Instead, he forced himself off the couch and went back to his kitchen table and looked through his latest findings. The murder had the look of another impulsive violent act. Gray was starting to think his first theory of an out-of-control killer might be accurate. He scratched his head as he tried to wrap his mind around the reasoning behind running over the animal. The perp stole what probably amounted to a few hundred dollars from the dealership's petty cash, but chose not to pick up an expensive tiara, even though he likely took the time to pick up his victim's shotgun. Was the perp just interested in building a body count? And why is the F.B.I. interested enough in this case to have its lead detective followed? Gray's head began to hurt as he tried to put together the pieces. He decided a good night's sleep might be needed after all, so he put his case notes away and grabbed some shuteye.

6

SHOPPIN' AT THE C.O.S.T.C.O.

When I awoke I felt refreshed. It was just after nine at night. The rest of my drive to the C.O.S.T.C.O. was incredibly peaceful. I drove down an old country road lush with wildlife. Massive trees and cuddly woodland creatures dominated this region of New Quebec. I took a long drag from a cigarette as I looked at all the wonderful scenery. It felt like a new world. A place where nature is respected and nurtured, not pillaged for profit. *As if a place like that ever existed*, I thought to myself as I tossed my cigarette butt out the driver-side window. Oh well, nothing wrong with a little wishful thinking, I suppose.

After an hour of driving I arrived at the C.O.S.T.C.O., New Quebec's bountiful black market. Although most items sold here are incredibly over-priced, the merchants believe in the barter system. People come here from all over the country to trade with this once-nomadic clan. The owners of the C.O.S.T.C.O. used to make their livings travelling from city to city all over the United States and Canada, committing small con jobs on unsuspecting boobs. After the merger of the countries, a crackdown on these travellers forced them to flee deep into the secluded forests of New Quebec. The local populous dubbed their place of business the C.O.S.T.C.O. These were definitely the people I needed to see.

I drove down a dirt path until I arrived at the front gate. A gate guard stepped out of his booth to ask what business I had within the walls of the centre. This man was obviously a warrior. The light from a torch showed his skin had the appearance of old leather and his face was riddled with scars. An automatic machine gun was clenched tightly in his hands. His clothes spoke of old battles. His green plaid jacket was covered in spatters of dry blood, and looked like it had been stitched up often enough to be tailor-made for Frankenstein. Many a blade must have attempted to enter the organs of this coat's wearer.

"Jimmy, get your stank ass outta my jacket!" ordered a familiar voice in an even more familiar angry tone.

I stuck my head outside the driver-side window to see who was treating this young soldier with such a lack of respect. My skull was introduced to the heel of a black riding boot.

When I awoke, I found myself laying face down on the dirt in front of my van. As I pulled myself to my feet, my jaw was greeted again — this time by a left jab and a right cross that sent me staggering back into the cattle-encrusted bumper still partially attached to my minivan.

"Hello there, asshole," said a sexy female voice. "I was beginning to think I'd never hear from you again."

I looked up and saw two fuzzy-looking women with flowing red locks and bright blue eyes standing in front of me. After my brain finished rattling around in my skull, the two women slowly merged into one clear figure — and what a figure! The young woman broke me out of my punch-drunk ogling with a stiff slap across my face.

"Snap out of it, jerk-off. What the hell are you doing here?" Kailey asked.

She appeared to become increasingly agitated every second I remained in her presence.

"I'm here to shop," I said, while rubbing my jaw. "By the way, why did you hit me? You on the rag or something?"

The fiery redhead responded by punching me in the kidneys, knocking me back onto the ground.

"Boy, I didn't think it would be possible, but you may actually be dumber than you look," she said while looking at me in disgust.

I decided now would be a wise time to attempt a peace treaty between us. "Please forgive me for my last remark," I said. "You're obviously feeling very sensitive right now. Can you tell me where we met?"

After I spoke I jumped to my feet, covering my face and kidneys.

"You seriously don't remember?" Kailey said with a look of disbelief.

"Sorry, I get hit in the head a lot."

"I'm somehow not surprised."

Kailey stretched her hand out towards me. This time there was no need for the whimpering and cowering I reacted with, although it did appear to entertain her.

"My name is Kailey," she said. "I kicked your ass for that stupid remark you made a few days ago at that shitty car lot in Old Toronto. I see you bought one of their top models. I hope this isn't what you're here to barter with."

I brushed off her crude remarks about my battle van as petty jealousy. After all, not everyone can own a sweet ride like my baby.

"No, no. The belly of this mighty beast holds my currency of choice," I said.

In truth, I did remember Kailey. My sudden amnesia was an attempt to weasel out of the money she wanted. Whoever heard of paying someone to replace the shoes they wore while they beat you? That's as ridiculous as a country charging prisoners rent for the cells they incarcerate them in.

"Just keep your tone nice and respectful like it is now and I won't have to turn your testes into a pair of earrings," she said.

This woman really likes to talk about my junk. I think she likes me.

"Fair enough, young maiden. Now can you please grant me access to the trading area?"

"Sure thing. As soon as you pay me for the shoes you ruined."

Shit. Maybe I can distract her with the old crazy routine.

"How could I wear your shoes? You're not even my size."

"What the hell are you talking about?"

"If boots are made for walking and that's just what they do, why do they have to walk all over people — I mean, they're doing what they were made to do. Shouldn't they be happy with that?"

Kailey's left eye began to twitch.

"And what about sandals and flip-flops," I added. "Are sandals more respected in the footwear world for sticking to their guns, while flip-flops can never seem to decide what side of the fence they're on?"

A vein began to pulse on the right side of Kailey's forehead.

"Tell you what," she said. "I'll forget about the shoes if you refrain from speaking with me for the rest of your visit."

"Sure, but that could make things awkward when I make sweet love to you."

Kailey's face turned white with anger. She turned around, took her jacket back from Jimmy, and began walking back to the main area of the trading centre.

She wants me.

I got back into my van and drove it into the central trading area. It was a large field that was hollowed out of the lush forest that sheltered the entire area. The trading floor was filled with pick-up trucks, vans, and tents. People from all over the continent had come to this den of sin to peddle wares to their fellow citizens. I pulled my trusty rolly-chair out of the back of my van and took a seat, and awaited my first customer.

* * * *

Monica Burke spent several hours looking over her notes and photos from the crime scenes, trying to draw some sort of connection between the victims. What was driving the killer? And who was this man from Washington? Was the suspect part of a nation-wide manhunt? Was the Washington man part of the F.B.I.? This had the potential to be a great front-page story, and she knew it. Monica called Gray's division from her living room apartment and left a message on his landline asking about potential involvement with the Feds out of Washington. She told him about the car with the Washington plates at both scenes and the mystery man behind the wheel. Monica knew Gray was unlikely to share any details about one of his open cases, but she also knew that if he was in a pissing match with an unhelpful federal officer he might release the Fed's information.

What do you know, Gray? Monica pondered to herself. She picked up the phone and ordered a pepperoni and mushroom pizza from Pookie's Pizzeria, then stretched out on her couch and closed her eyes. "Maybe things will be clearer after pizza," she said to herself as she settled down for a catnap.

* * * *

As Gray approached his captain's office at 6 a.m. the following morning, he was instantly glad he got a decent night's sleep. The F.B.I. agent he embarrassed and assaulted the night before was already in Gleeb's office. Gray could hear muffled words like "suspension" and "misconduct" coming from the agent's mouth and bouncing off the glass walls of his captain's office.

Gray didn't hesitate when he reached the office door. He opened it up as the two men were in mid-discussion and slammed it behind him.

"Am I late for the party, gentlemen?" Gray asked.

"Don't you know how to knock, detective?" Spacek asked.

"Agent Spacek, I didn't recognize you without your camera lurking in the shadows."

"Kiss my ass, Gray, you—"

"Enough you two," Gleeb said. "You sound like my pain-in-the-ass kids. Now Gray, Spacek was just about to inform me as to why he was following you last night."

"Captain Gleeb, that is hardly why I'm here. That information is classified. I'm here to file an official complaint against your detective for assault."

"Like hell you are," Gleeb said before Gray could respond. "You're lucky my man didn't plug you full of holes for trying that spook shit on him. I don't appreciate my men being followed around without my authorization. Why don't you tell us what the hell you're doing in our neck of the woods?"

Gray was impressed by his captain's fire. He hadn't seen Gleeb this angry since the doughnut shop down the street was shut down for three weeks for renovations. Gleeb really loves their sugar twists.

Spacek looked annoyed, but he opened up a leather satchel, removed a manila file and handed it to Captain Gleeb.

"The contents of this file do not leave the eyes of the people in this room," Spacek said.

Gray nodded in agreement, curious to see what the agent was carrying. Gleeb looked at the contents of the folder briefly before handing them to Gray. The detective skimmed through the folder. It was filled with poorly written police reports from gruesome murders across the country, including a double homicide in Florida where the attacker beat an elderly couple to death with a claw hammer; the hit-and-run death of a

36-year-old man in Iowa; the stabbing death of a homeless man in New York and a man tossed out of a seventh-floor window of an apartment in Las Vegas.

"These crimes don't look related," Gray said. "Why are they filed together?"

"Because looks can be deceiving, detective," said Spacek. "The bureau has reason to believe these crimes are connected and that our killer was headed towards Toronto a few days ago."

"Jesus! And you're telling us this now?" Gleeb said. "We could have had men out on the streets looking for this psychopath."

"That's the Feds for you, Captain," Gray said. "They don't like other people playing in their sandbox."

"For your information, detective, we have a team of more than a dozen agents across the country compiling information on our suspect. The randomness and viciousness of these latest crimes in the Toronto area fit our killer's M.O."

"Based on these notes, so far all you've shown us are a handful of random crimes with nothing tying them to our suspect. I find it depressing that this is what passes for note-taking in other jurisdictions. And who's doing the profiling on this? Why didn't they press the local police for more details?" Gray asked, annoyed with the lazy incompetence of his fellow officers. "Captain, the F.B.I.'s file could have multiple killers. There's a serious lack of evidence here to allow us to connect these deaths. I don't see any connections between them or with our suspect. Unless the F.B.I. isn't telling us something, I think they're wasting our time"

"Our suspect? So you believe the killings in the car lot and at the dairy farm are connected?" Gleeb asked.

"Yes, sir. Windshield glass found on the scene at the dairy farm matches the glass type used on the van taken from the lot. Also, the perp is showing the same kind of violent impulses at both scenes," Gray replied.

"The tire treads also match," said a muzzled voice from the other side of the door. It was Crump. He was standing by the office door eavesdropping, while munching away on a honey-glazed doughnut.

"How long has that man been standing there?" asked Spacek.

"Doesn't matter, he's my partner on this," Gray replied as he motioned for Crump to enter the office.

Crump introduced himself to Spacek who rolled his eyes in response, ignoring the rookie.

"Look, gentlemen, all these crimes are connected," Spacek said.

"How do you know that for sure?" Gray asked.

"Because of the car found on your murder scene at the used car lot," he replied.

"That shit box didn't match to any of the car lot's records?" Crump said. "It didn't have a V.I.N. number or any other way to identify the owner. The licence plates were fakes."

Gray quickly skimmed through the F.B.I. file again.

"Son of a bitch," he said. "It's the car model identified in the Florida murder."

"And the hit-and-run," added Spacek. "We figure he was doing a car dump to keep authorities from connecting the killings."

"Do you have an I.D. yet?" Gray asked.

"No. This guy knows how to keep a low profile. We haven't been able to compile any sort of physical description. We figure he's hiding in plain sight."

"These latest crime scenes have been pretty messy. If this is your perp, he's getting sloppy," Gleeb said.

"We think something has changed recently to make him more erratic. That should make him easier to catch this time," Spacek replied.

"It also makes him more dangerous," added Gray.

"Where do you think he's headed next?" Crump asked.

"We believe he will attempt to flee the country to avoid arrest," Spacek said. "Quickest way to disappear from here is to head into New Quebec."

"Plenty of opportunity there to pick up fake passports, hop aboard a ship and sail into international waters," Gray said.

"Which is partially why I was following you last night, detective," Spacek replied.

"Come again?" Gray said.

"I've been watching you, and your methods. The Bureau thinks you would make a useful asset for tracking down our suspect over the border."

"Why doesn't the F.B.I. just go hunt him down?" Crump asked as he pulled out his phone and snapped a picture of Spacek. Spacek showed Crump his middle finger in response.

"The F.B.I. wants to maintain the illusion that Glamerica respects New Quebec's open-border policy with us," Gray said. "It's a lot easier to send a couple of over-zealous local cops over the border after a suspect. That way if we mess up, the Bureau can hang a couple of cops out to dry instead of creating an international incident. Am I wrong, Agent Spacek?"

"The New Quebec government prefers to limit the number of Glamerican law enforcement agents that enter its borders," Spacek replied. "It prefers to police its problems itself, detective. But since this killer is a Glamerican citizen, its government should be a little more forgiving of a couple of detectives from the TPD crossing its border and apprehending a dangerous killer without permission — if those detectives were to be discovered."

"Why keep this so hush-hush?" Crump asked.

"Because Glamerica polices its own as well, detective," Spacek replied. "We are the leaders of this world. We don't need help from our weaker allies to deal with domestic issues. Anyway, my superiors will authorize the TPD sending in a couple of men. After last night I was going to cross Gray off my list, but since you seem to have ample faith in his abilities, Captain Gleeb, I am willing to give him a chance."

Gleeb nodded, picked up the phone and looked at Gray.

"I'll make a few calls and get you two set up with false identifications and a car for your trip," said Gleeb.

"You sure about this, Captain? It's a big risk for our department," Gray said.

"Go pack your bags," Gleeb replied. "You're going after this bastard."

Gray grabbed his files on the suspect, then hopped in his car and took off. As he drove home to pack for his trip, he tried to put together the pieces of the puzzle that Spacek gave him during their latest encounter. Were the crimes the F.B.I. agent listed actually connected to his killer? If so, why did Spacek follow Gray in secret and not just enlist the services of the TPD? Were these the actions of one rogue government agent looking to prove himself to his superiors by stealing the hard investigative work of others, and keeping all the credit for a major bust for himself? It wouldn't have been the first time, Gray thought as he approached his condo building. Still, something stunk about Spacek. There were pieces of the puzzle still missing and either Spacek wasn't interested in sharing them, or he didn't have them himself. Either way, Gray thought he was a Grade-A asshole. However, if all the crimes were indeed connected, the killer may prove to be extremely elusive, even for Gray.

Suspect : Unknown

Gender : Male

Description:
- Tall, Caucasian, "scraggy-looking," unshaven
- Wearing dark jacket, possibly covered in oil

Behaviour:
- Prone to impulsive, violent acts → cruel to animals
- May see crimes as a game (I.O.U left at scene)
- Possible spree killer/serial killer
- Left 10K tiara behind; robbery is an unlikely motive
- Successfully eluded feds; must assume is highly intelligent

Additional notes:
- Suspect may have mechanical background
- Driving stolen van (silver) → glass at farmhouse match
- Size 10 sneaker prints found at crime scene
- Possibly armed with shotgun
- Attempting to flee country through New Quebec?

* * * *

After a long night of twiddling my thumbs and napping, my first potential C.O.S.T.C.O. customer arrived at 7:30 a.m. It was a small elderly woman interested in obtaining a rocking chair. Fortunately, I packed my grandmother's old rocker into the van. I hope Granny doesn't mind. After all, she did leave it at my place when she broke her hip and ended up in the hospital. I pulled the wooden rocker out of the van and placed it next to the old woman so her booty could give it a seal of approval. She let out a relieving sigh as she sat in the chair, her bones crackling from every laboured movement.

"Now this is a nice chair," the woman said. "What would you like in exchange for it?"

The elderly woman looked up at me and smiled. What a sweet old lady, I thought to myself. She probably wants to trade me a knitted sweater or a batch of cookies for it.

"Well now, let's just see what you have to offer and we can take it from there," I replied in a soft, respectful tone.

"You are such a sweet young man. I'll have my granddaughter bring my things around for you to see. Kailey, come help this young gentleman."

Kailey?

I turned my head and watched the fiery redhead I encountered earlier stroll up to my van and greet her grandmother with a peck on the cheek. She was carrying a silver briefcase in her right arm.

"Hi, Grammy. So where's this young gentleman you want me to help?" she said, shortly before looking right through me with a cold glare.

"Right here, dear," the old woman said while motioning towards me, much to Kailey's dismay. "This polite young man wants to trade me his rocking chair."

Kailey forced her succulent lips to produce a big, customer service-style smile. She would be feeling the effects of that grin in the morning.

"So what are you interested in, sir?" she asked as she grit her teeth.

"Well now, I can certainly see where your granddaughter gets her radiant beauty from," I said, eliciting a giggle from Grammy. Kailey's eye began to twitch again.

"You see now, dear, this is the kind of man that is husband material," Grammy said. "You two should go out sometime."

Kailey attempted to maintain her composure in front of her grandmother. Whenever her elder had her back towards me, I would send Kailey out a love vibe, expressing my romantic interests through the gift of sign, the most powerful of all languages that woo. First, I caught her attention by pointing at her and then back at myself and offered a flirtatious smile. Kailey looked confused, so to ensure there was no miscommunication, I made orgasmic faces as I sensually grinded the air with my arms outstretched as if they had a firm grasp of Kailey's waist and her long red locks. She looked hot and bothered, or just bothered — I've never been good at differentiating the two. When Kailey's grandmother faced me again, I was standing up straight with perfect posture and my hands were sitting at my sides like an attentive Boy Scout awaiting orders. Grammy definitely would have let me help her cross the street. Kailey returned my affections with her own sign language. Although she was obviously a beginner in the language of love fingers, I was able to decode her romantic message. Her first gestures were to bat her eyelashes at me, smile, and make a fist with her thumb sticking out. It was a little Fonzian, but I played along. Next, she put her thumb up to her right ear and slid it across her throat to her left ear. This was obviously her way of telling me that she wants my hands wrapped around her neck in a loving embrace. Pretty hot.

"Let me show you our wares, kind sir," said Kailey.

She rested her briefcase on the stump of an old tree. When the case opened, it displayed a wide range of espionage equipment.

"I worked for the secret service in my youth, sonny," Grammy whispered. "But don't tell anyone — it's a secret."

I knelt down and whispered back in her ear.

"Don't worry, your secret is safe with me."

Grammy smiled.

"I knew I could trust you, sonny, that's why I told you. Of course, if you were to leak that info I could still take you out."

"I don't doubt that, ma'am."

"Good thing, kiddo. I may be old, but I can still snap a neck in two seconds flat."

I gave Grammy a wide-eyed smile and a polite nod. Wow! A killer grandma. Cool. You don't meet one of those every day. I stood back up and turned my attention to Kailey.

"Alright, little missy, let's see your goods."

Kailey was not amused.

"They're my Grammy's goods, just so we're clear."

"Oh, well, let's see what Grammy is packing. I mean, let's trade."

Kailey went through each item as if she was offering up the features of a new car. She was a hell of a saleswoman; Sal would have been proud.

"I'll trade you three of the following items for the chair: one piece of plastic explosive gum with foil detonator, a pair of night vision goggles, a 9mm machine gun with silencer, a military-grade sniper rifle, a box of waterproof matches, a glassblower whistle, or a fake wax moustache."

I couldn't believe that a rocking chair could be worth so much to one person. This must be my lucky day. Picking the first two items was a no-brainer.

"I'll take the fake moustache and the waterproof matches."

Kailey raised an eyebrow for a moment, then removed the moustache and matches from the display and tossed them into my hands. The final item was a tough call, since they were all potentially useful. I knew that because of all the old spy movies I watched as a child. If it was good enough for secret agents like 008 and the legendary *69, then how could I turn up my nose at any of them? The only item I had never seen in the movies was the glassblowing whistle.

"So what exactly does the glassblower do?"

"Let me show you, sir," Kailey said as she snatched the whistle from the case and strolled over to the front of my van. "Watch and learn."

She pressed the whistle up to her luscious lips and, without a sound, my van's remaining windows were completely shattered, leaving the seats littered with broken glass. Well, at least the name doesn't lie, I thought to myself. That whistle definitely blows. Kailey walked back to her Grammy's briefcase and awaited my response.

"Hmm, tempting. But I think I'll go with the night vision goggles," I said as I grabbed the goggles and placed them on my head. Kailey stared in disbelief. This woman really liked to stare at me. Not that I could blame her; I am one hot piece of ass. I thanked the two women for the transaction and gave Kailey's Grammy a kiss on the cheek. Kailey rolled her eyes and turned away.

"Now, now dear," Kailey's Grammy said. "Let this gentleman give you a little kiss."

Kailey turned her head back towards her grandmother just long enough for me to plant one right on her lips. Grammy giggled while Kailey stood frozen, obviously in shock from our electricity.

"See you later, ladies," I said.

"You should go after that man," Grammy said to her red-headed bundle of joy.

"Don't you worry, Grammy, he'll be seeing me again real soon."

I knew Kailey had feelings for me. My chest burned as I watched the redhead pack up her grandmother's things and walk away, disappearing from my line of sight. I knew I shouldn't have eaten that old man's hotdog.

7

BUILDING a FOLLOWING

Gray and Crump packed up their necessary equipment and met back at Division 22 at 9 a.m. They jumped in an unmarked blue sedan and began their trip towards the New Quebec border. Crump began reading the front page story of the Gazette, but stopped halfway through.

"What happened to our favourite saucy little reporter? Has she been pulled off the case?" Crump asked as he put his cellphone in his pocket.

"What are you talking about?" Gray asked.

"Monica's byline isn't on the front page story covering the Car Lot Killer. It's someone named Johnson Nash. And it's more of a re-hash of old events and press releases than a new story."

"He's the editor of the paper. Maybe Monica got burned by a source and they had to pull her piece."

"Yeah, well, karma is a bitch like that."

Crump disliked reporters in general, which created a conflict for him since he had a raging hard-on for Monica. Most people saw it as the common love-hate relationship that exists between many police officers and reporters. Gray knew it ran deeper than that for the rookie detective. Crump got dumped after a hot, two-month fling with the reporter. The young rookie's ego never fully recovered.

Before hopping on Highway 401 East, Gray made a pit stop at the courthouse to pay a visit to D.A. Helmer's office.

"Why are we stopping here?" asked Crump.

"I need to let Helmer know what's going on — just in case."

"Just in case of what?"

"In case things turn south."

"Why? Wouldn't he hang us out to dry to save his skin?"

"Maybe. But the city needs to have its top prosecutor prepared to deflect the media frenzy that would ensue if we screw this up. No reason for the city to go down with our ship."

Crump scratched his scalp before shrugging his shoulders as a sign of accepting Gray's explanation. Gray parked in front of the courthouse in a loading zone and jumped out of the car.

"I'll be back in ten minutes. Stay in the car, in case someone needs us to move it."

"Sure thing, boss. Can you bring me back a doughnut? A chocolate éclair, maybe?"

"You ate a sugar twist and a raspberry jelly while we were loading the car. Give your heart a rest."

"Don't worry, boss, I run off this stuff. It keeps me sharp," Crump said while pointing at his head.

"It keeps you soft," Gray replied while pointing to his partner's belly. Crump wasn't overweight, but he had a soft middle. The cream puff, as Gray liked to describe it. When he was a boxer, he always made his opponents pay if they entered the ring with a soft middle. Gray would work their bodies until they folded like an accordion.

"This is just more of me to love," Crump said while grabbing part of his mushy midsection. "You've got to give the ladies a comfortable pillow for when they're working you south of the border."

"You're a true gentleman. No doughnuts. I'll be back in ten."

"You're the boss."

Although Gray did not agree with all of the district attorney's antics, he did believe in extending professional courtesy to his crime fighting colleagues whenever possible. Gray was a firm believer that cracks and divisions within the city's criminal justice system would only serve as advantages to the criminals they were all trying to lock up. He tried to remember that whenever he had dealings with the F.B.I., but after several blown cases due to federal interference and miscommunication, Gray found the organization more of a hindrance than a help. They were a bunch of cowboys who wanted all the glory. They were too quick to shut out local detectives that spent weeks, sometimes months, working scenes, finding clues and generating leads. When Gray arrived at Helmer's office, he turned down offers of a Cuban cigar and a cappuccino before getting down to business.

"I appreciate you coming to me with this, Sandman," Helmer said. "Personally, I don't trust the feds. Those bastards will throw us under a bus with the first sniff of bad press. You and your partner better watch your asses."

"Agreed."

"So what's your cover?"

"Crump and I are two run-of-the-mill degenerate gamblers looking for a weekend of ill repute over the border."

Helmer laughed and let out a small snort.

"That kind of role doesn't really suit you, Gray. Of course, your young partner will probably be able to sell both of you as degenerates simultaneously."

"He's got talent. He'll make a good detective once he grows out of his stupid."

"We were all young once, I suppose."

"Exactly. He'll come around."

"With you on his ass I don't doubt that. Try and keep me informed if at all possible as the case progresses. I want to make sure I can pull you guys out of there if things get too hot."

Gray smirked and nodded. He stood up and shook Helmer's hand before exiting his office.

"Thanks, Helmer. Keep fighting the good fight."

"Always. Go get this psycho."

Gray walked by the courthouse cafeteria on his way out. He saw his young partner stuffing a doughnut into his mouth while simultaneously slurping a large coffee. Crump noticed him and gave him a smile. Crump looked like a hamster that had stuffed its cheeks full of sunflower seeds.

"Hey, boss, so is everything kosher?" Crump said while spraying coffee-drenched doughnut spittle onto Gray's shoes.

Gray stared back at him without a word. Crump quickly swallowed and wiped his mouth on his sleeve. "Sorry, boss. So, are we good to go?"

"Jesus, Crump, did you really need a third doughnut that badly?"

"If I didn't eat the third one, how could I eat the fourth?" he said while extending a half-eaten doughnut towards Gray. "Bite?"

"Just get in the car, rookie."

As the two detectives walked to their car, Gray noticed a parking ticket stuck to the driver-side wiper blade. He removed it and handed it to Crump.

"Hope you liked those doughnuts, kid. They just cost you ninety-five bucks."

Crump swore to himself and shoved the ticket into his pocket before getting into the car and starting their drive towards the onramp for the highway. A black SUV sitting across the street from the courthouse started its engine and began tailing the detectives at a distance.

* * * *

I fought through my heartburn and removed the remaining furniture from my van. I still had a pullout couch and a lamp shaped like a football to sell. I decided I would try and keep the pullout couch as a place to rest my weary bones over the course of what would likely be my last road trip. After sweeping out most of the broken glass from the van, I decided to assess my battlewagon's road worthiness. The van had a gaping hole created by the grizzly moose that needed to be repaired before I headed back to Glamerica. My battlewagon needed to be in tip top shape if I was to succeed in my mission. It must be repaired with great haste. Who knew how much time was left? I was so focused on the fate of both my van and my mission, I didn't notice a burly old man in greasy overalls and a bright yellow trucker's hat walking towards me. He came to an abrupt halt when he saw the condition of my van.

"Well I'll be a salamander's uncle wearing spandex on a Sunday! Now that is what I call vehicular homicide," the old man said while letting out a belly-jiggling burst of laughter.

He moved his head up and down, continuing to assess my vehicle. He rubbed his unshaven chin and placed his hands on his sides, which over the course of his life had been upgraded from love handles to love sofas. Maybe if I sweet talk him he will give me the name of a mechanic in the area, I thought.

"Do you know anyone who can fix all this damage or are you just here for some friendly chit-chat, my little grease dumpling?" I asked while giving him a wink and a smile.

The old man removed his hat and smiled back at me. His face was flush with embarrassment, a more positive response than I anticipated.

"Now don't you be playing with the emotions of ol' Jeremiah if you ain't truly feelin' his vibe," the old man said as he rubbed his chest.

"I might be feelin' your vibe if you can get this here van a new back door and windshield," I replied.

Jeremiah threw his hat to the ground and performed what appeared to be a hillbilly victory dance.

"Hot-diggity-ding-dang-do! You come back in an hour and I'll have this bird ready to fly. Yee-haw!"

Well, that was simple.

"No problem, Jeremiah. See you in an hour. By the way, what do you want in return for the parts and labour?"

"I'll take that football lamp, the rolling chair and the couch for the parts. As for the labour, I'm sure we can work something out," he said while sliding his tongue across his wind-burned lips.

This was not a good trade — for many reasons — but what choice did I have? I forced my face to smile as I attempted to make a counter-offer.

"Tell you what, Jeremiah. You can have all the furniture except for the chair with the wheels. Is that fair?"

"Yeah, I guess that's fine. I don't have much use for a chair like that anyhow."

"Alright then, I'll be back in a couple of hours. But for now, I have to roll."

I hopped onto my chair and rolled away from the greasy mechanic towards a scenic walking path. I could feel his eyes undressing me from behind. God I hope I can get the van from him without paying for the labour. He's not even my type.

* * * *

After a slow, painful morning crawl across the city, Gray and Crump barrelled down the highway. They shot passed Cobourg, Belleville, Kingston and Cornwall in four hours as they approached the unmanned border of New Quebec. They pulled over at a rest area for a quick refuel and caffeinated recharge.

Gray drove up to the self-service gas pumps and hopped out of the car. Crump got out of the vehicle and stretched his arms into the air. His back cracked loudly, catching Gray's attention.

"Rookie, are you twenty-five going on eighty?"

Crump replied with a toothy smile. "I'm going inside to grab some grub. You want anything, bossman?"

Gray ignored the bossman comment and began pumping gas.

"Just a coffee for me. Black. Don't get too many doughnuts. I don't want you slowing our car down with your fat ass."

"Don't hate the booty, boss. The chicks dig it," Crump said as he made his way inside the station's store.

Gray took a moment while refuelling to take in the beautiful scenery. He was surrounded by lush forests that somehow continued to thrive despite decades of lax pollution laws. Gray tried to take a deep breath of fresh air, but the foul odour emanating from the paper and pulp mills just across the border made him cough.

"This is the wrong spot to be breathing like that, friend," said an old man holding a jug of bleach and a metal spatula. "It's like being downwind from a bean-eating contest."

"Agreed," Gray replied.

"You and that young fella heading to New Quebec for a little fun?"

"Yes, we are looking to do a lot of drinking and gambling."

The old man looked Gray up and down and raised an eyebrow.

"You don't look like much of a partier to me. More like a bible salesman, except for the muscles. You one of them pro fighter-turned-Jesus types?"

"That's 'cause you haven't seen him with a forty and some powder," Crump said as he returned to the car with a tray of coffees and a box of doughnuts. "I've personally seen this man take a line of blow off a stripper's ass while getting a shotgun from a whore and playing six simultaneous games of online poker. I won't even get into what happens once the pepperoni pizza arrives."

The old man gave both men a disapproving shake of his head before walking away. Gray took a moment to stare at Crump.

"Rookie, if I ever make the Monday-morning mistake of asking you how you spent your weekend, please remind me of the conversation that just took place."

"C'mon, Gray, you know I'm just in character. Enjoy your coffee and have a doughnut," Crump replied while pushing the tray of coffees and box of assorted doughnuts into Gray's shoulder. Gray pushed the doughnuts away, grabbed his coffee and jumped into the car. He was about to begin the drive over the border when he spotted a black SUV in the parking lot by the store.

"Crump, see that black SUV?"

The young detective was already face-deep in doughnut when he looked in the rear-view mirror.

"Yeah, what's up?"

"There was a black SUV at the courthouse earlier today, and I think I saw one on our way through Cobourg. I think we're being followed. I want you to get out and walk back to the store. If it tries to take off, I'll block the SUV in with the car."

"But I was just there, boss. What reason would I have for going back?" Crump asked as he raised a raspberry jelly-filled doughnut towards his mouth.

Gray fired a lightning-fast jab with his right hand into the doughnut, splattering jelly all over the young detective's T-shirt and face.

"Looks like you need some napkins, rookie."

It took a few seconds for Crump to shake off the shock from Gray's surprise doughnut attack and respond.

"Not cool, Gray. Not cool at all," he said as he got out of the car and began walking back to the store. He took his shirt off and began wiping his face with the remaining clean areas on it.

His shirtless body exposed muscular shoulders and arms and a pudgy midsection. Crump continued to lift weights to impress the ladies at the bars he frequented, but had let himself get behind on his cardio workouts since passing his last department physical. He had a tattoo of a cartoon milkshake on the back of his right shoulder. He had told Gray once that it was from his favourite cartoon growing up. The veteran detective told Crump he was an idiot for getting it.

Gray kept the car idling as he watched Crump make his way to the store. The black SUV started to reverse out of its spot as Crump approached the lot, so Gray put his car in reverse and put his foot to the floor, screeching the tires as the vehicle sped backwards into the parking lot entrance. The SUV's driver tried to escape but Gray successfully blocked his path. The mystery driver slammed on the brakes, narrowly avoiding a collision. Crump ran up to the SUV's driver-side window, aimed his pistol at the driver's head and began yelling orders.

"Show me your hands — and some napkins!"

Gray jumped out of the car and removed his pistol from its holster.

The driver raised his hands and awaited further instructions. He had long, greasy hair that curled out of his ballcap and covered most of his face. His eyes were hidden behind oversized aviator sunglasses. Crump opened the door and instructed the driver to get out of the vehicle. As the mystery man got out of the car, Gray instantly recognized the creep behind the costume and holstered his weapon.

"Nice costume, Spacek. Did the F.B.I. run out of department-issued glasses with fake noses?"

"Fuck you, Gray," Spacek said as he took off his disguise. "Did you really think I would let you take the credit for this bust after what you pulled on me?"

Crump lowered his weapon. His face turned red from embarrassment over not recognizing the F.B.I. agent.

"But what about limiting Glamerican involvement?" Crump asked.

"The feds won't care as long as the killer is caught and everything goes smoothly," Gray explained. "Of course if this goes south Spacek will still try and sell us out."

"Eat me, Gray," Spacek replied. "If this goes south we're all in deep shit. Turns out it's a good thing I was following you. I was just informed by my superiors that Detective Crump is needed back in Toronto."

"You've got to be shitting me," the rookie replied.

"Mind your tongue, detective," Spacek snapped back. "One of your contacts back home has been assaulted. A reporter named Monica Burke."

Crump's face went white with adrenelin. Gray could see his partner's face filling with both fear and anger.

"When did this happen?" Gray asked.

"Sometime last night during a break-in at her apartment. She was found in her pajamas unconscious, beaten and bloody."

"Jesus," Crump replied. "Was it some perv?"

"The rape kit is being processed now, but the techs on scene think it's unlikely. Looks like the perp took off with her purse, computer and a few other small electronic devices."

"So if it's a simple smash 'n' grab, why send me home?" Crump asked.

"Because detective, your captain isn't convinced it's that simple. He wants you to get down to the hospital and interview her to see if there is any connection to the stories she has been writing. If she wakes up."

"It's that bad?" Crump asked with dread in his voice.

"Looks that way, detective. She was slowly bleeding out from a stab wound when her editor came by her place to see why she didn't show up for work. The docs are giving her a fifty/fifty shot. Gleeb wants you there if she wakes up because he figures the reporter will cooperate with you given your personal history.

Your superiors informed me you dated. And since I need Gray's tracking and profiling ability to continue the manhunt for our killer, that makes you the right man for the job."

Crump turned to Gray to hear his input.

"It makes sense, rookie. If the attack is somehow connected, we need to know. If Monica pulls through she could I.D. the attacker."

Crump nodded, a little disappointed with his mentor's answer, but relieved he could go check on Monica.

"Yeah, I guess that's true. But you can't go hunting this guy by yourself."

Spacek tossed his keys for the SUV to Crump.

"Take my vehicle back to the station and check in with your superiors. I will continue the investigation with Detective Gray," Spacek said as his cellphone rang. "Excuse me for a minute, gentleman," he said as he took a few steps away from the detectives.

Crump gave Gray a look of uncertainty and discomfort. Gray gave the rookie a reassuring nod.

"It'll be fine, kid. Don't worry, I'll keep you in the loop. Let me know what you find out about Monica's attacker," Gray said just out of earshot from Spacek.

"Sure thing, boss. Be careful. I don't trust this guy."

"Always, rookie."

Crump nodded, grabbing a clean death metal t-shirt from the back of Gray's car before jumping into the black SUV. He quickly put on the shirt, tossing his jelly-stained shirt in the back. Gray hopped into the sedan and moved it forward. Crump drove out of the lot and began driving back towards Toronto. Spacek opened the front passenger door to Gray's sedan and hopped inside.

"We should leave immediately, detective," Spacek said. "I was just informed that our suspect might have been spotted at a maple farm, just a few hours from the trading centre."

Gray nodded and peeled the car out of the rest area into New Quebec.

8

a love rolly-coaster

My trusty rolly chair was never for sale. I have too many fond memories of racing down the hallways of my apartment drunk as a skunk in it. Rose and I regularly enjoy rolly-chair races after long nights of drinking. The goal is to be the first person to roll down the stairs to the first-floor lobby without wiping out. It has always been a work in progress. Rose holds the record of most steps without falling. She was able to make it down six of the eighty-two steps. Rose always beat me. I suspect she played this game prior to our friendship. That's okay. She'll need all her skills for the next time we meet; if there ever is a next time.

As I rolled my way through throngs of excited C.O.S.T.C.O. consumers, I stumbled upon a steep, narrow, dirt path — must have been a good fifty-metre drop, practically straight down. The path appeared to end close to a section of dense forest. There was no way I would be able to stop my chair in time. And the "stop, drop and roll" method of breaking didn't look all that appealing, especially sober.

"Too steep for me," I said to myself, as I tried to slowly roll away from the edge of the path. But my chair suddenly stopped.

"Oh I beg to differ, dipshit. I think that path is perfectly steep for you!"

I swiveled my plastic chariot around and saw Kailey standing in front of me. She smiled as she placed the toe of her boot between my legs on the rolly-chair, revealing a beautifully sculpted leg and a small peek at her shimmering purple thong. I just sat there slack-jawed as Kailey raised her lovely left brow and smirked as she gently pushed my chair, sending me rolling backwards down the steep path. It took a few seconds for my brain to shake off the wonderful image of Kailey's underpants and realize the peril I was in. I was rolling towards a horde of trees at a speed of too-many-kilometres per hour. While rocketing towards my doom, one of the chair's wheels hit a small bump in the path, almost launching me completely off my chair. Luckily, my cat-like reflexes allowed me to quickly grip the sides of the seat, which swivelled forward. I let out a sharp scream as I drew closer to the dense collection of trees.

Narrowly avoiding the first twenty feet of living lumber, I spun past them while struggling to maintain balance on the bumpy trail. My ride down the hill ended abruptly when the wheels of my chair got snagged in the roots of a large tree. Since my hands had a fear-filled, ironclad grip on the sides of the seat, it was ejected along with yours truly. I shot up into the air like a fighter pilot ejecting from a downed aircraft. My head and shoulders worked like a battering ram, smashing through branches and leaves until I was free of the forest and shooting through the sky. I sailed over blurry patches of green, tightly grasping the seat cushion until gravity caught up to me. Trying my best to mimic a scared turtle, I tucked my body onto the chair, shut my eyes and braced for impact. As the chair hit the ground I felt a splash of something moist hit my face. I opened my eyes and watched in delight as I skidded across a lake of shimmering blue water. A double win! Not only had I cheated certain death, but I was also pretty sure the moistness wasn't coming from me.

I figured I would hold on tight to my seat until the lake came to a complete stop. I figured wrong. The seat quickly broke into several pieces, sending me skipping across the water until I bounced onto the shore, slid through a puddle of mud and came to a bone-rattling stop at the trunk of a large tree. Everything went dark.

When I awoke, it took me a few moments to gain my bearings. I looked around and did a quick assessment of my bruised, bloody and muddy body. I was able to move all my bits and pieces, so I decided there was at least a sixty-five per cent chance I was still alive. I gripped on to a thick branch from the tree I collided with and painfully pulled myself to my feet. The air felt clean and was a welcome addition to my lungs. I dug through my pockets and pulled out a beat-up, foil pack of cigarettes. I pulled out a half-broken smoke, lit it with my new waterproof matches, and laughed in the face of death.

"Ha! Is that the best you can do?" I yelled into the sky.

I pulled a drag from my smoke and gave the tree a kick. I did not notice the bee hive hanging precariously above my head on a broken branch. The collision must have knocked the hive loose from its home and awoken the horde of angry bees that now circled, looking for a reason to sting. My kick had just enough force to release the hive from its branch. It dropped straight down and found a new home on the top of my head. I sprinted back towards the water, flailing my arms around like a man, well, like a man with a beehive attached to his head. I lunged into the lake and swam deep into the dark water until the hive and bees came loose. As I made my way back to the surface, I could feel the top of my head beginning to swell. I swam across the lake and headed back in the direction of the narrow, dirt path that led back into the trading area. As I made my way out of the lake and climbed up the path, the pain from my tenderized torso and swollen skull retreated into the back of my mind as my thoughts were overcome again with a heavenly image. Mmm, purple.

* * * *

Spacek and Gray took the NQ-40 West to the NQ-15 North and shot through Boisbriand and St. Jerome, towards a maple tree farm just outside Mont Tremblant. Neither one seemed particularly interested in small talk. Outside of Spacek's phone call with local law enforcement where he obtained a few of the details from the responding officer at the maple farm, the two men drove in silence until they approached the crime scene around 3:15 p.m.

"I thought we were supposed to keep our presence here a secret," Gray said.

"Sylvain is an old friend and ally. He'll keep our presence quiet," Spacek replied. Gray nodded in response.

"So what are we looking at here — another murder?" Gray asked.

"No. The security guard at the Sticky Tree Maple Farm foiled a robbery early yesterday morning by a suspect driving a vehicle that fits the description of the stolen van."

"A robbery?"

"Yeah, apparently our guy covered himself with mud and sticks, snuck into the grounds and attempted to steal some of the tree sap. One of the guards spotted him and sicked a grizzly moose on him."

"Another miracle of modern science," Gray said in a sarcastic tone.

"The animal attacked the van, tearing one of the doors clean off. The guard heard what he thought was a shotgun blast, and then the animal stopped dead in its tracks."

"Killed?"

"Nope. It was stopped by a splinter in its paw. The perp had the van loaded to the tits with furniture. A bookshelf, a desk and a few other items fell out of it and smashed on the ground."

Gray felt confused. It didn't fit the profile of the killer to risk getting caught for petty theft when he already appeared to be murdering people whenever the opportunity arose. It wouldn't have the same kind of risk associated with it. Where was the thrill? But those thoughts quickly left him when he heard about the lost personal effects.

"Did the desk have anything interesting inside it?" he asked.

"Not sure. The guys on the scene were told to stop mucking around after we found out it could be our guy."

Gray took the NQ-117 West until he hit the exit marked "Sticky Tree Maple Farm" and followed a dirt path downhill until he came to a line of yellow tape and a dozen members of local law enforcement.

"Looks like the gang is all here," Spacek said while smirking.

"I just hope they haven't compromised the scene," Gray replied as he parked on the side of the road.

The two men got out of the car and walked towards the crime tape. Gray showed his badge to one of the officers, figuring his cover was already blown thanks to the F.B.I. The officer was short, balding and overweight. He responded by crossing his arms and snorting.

"That badge won't do you too much good here. This is not your home," the officer said in a snarky French accent.

"What about this one?" Spacek said as he flashed his F.B.I. badge. "Sergeant Sylvain Paperneau let me know where to find you guys."

The officer nodded and lifted the tape, welcoming the two men inside. Spacek was greeted by an older man in a green windbreaker and blue jeans.

The two men shook hands, then Spacek introduced Gray to the police sergeant.

"Thank you both for coming. I'm not sure what to make of this mess," said Paperneau.

"Anytime, old friend. Thanks for letting us know about the potential lead," replied Spacek.

The three men walked towards the scene of the crime, where pieces of broken furniture were scattered across the dirt road.

"Was there anything of interest inside the furniture?" asked Gray.

"Maybe. But we have left that for you to sort out. I have enough on my plate without worrying about another country's criminals," Paperneau replied while motioning to one of his officers. The officer came forward with a cardboard box and handed it to Gray.

"This is everything we collected from the scene — mostly papers and the odd knick-knack," Paperneau said. "We didn't want any of it to blow away or be destroyed by the mud."

"Where is the security guard that witnessed the robbery?" asked Gray.

"I'll take you to him right now," Paperneau replied.

"Check it out," said Spacek. "I'll search through the papers to see if there is anything that will help us."

"You don't want to interview the witness?" Gray said, surprised at his new partner's response.

"You do this for a living, too, don't you detective?" he replied in a snarky tone. "The perp has a lead on us. We need to find him as quickly as possible. We need to divide and conquer."

He took the box from Gray and began walking back to the car.

"Spacek's actually a very helpful resource, when he's not being a total asshole," Paperneau whispered, making Gray smirk. "C'mon, Captain Glamerica, let's go introduce you to the hero of the day."

Gray followed Paperneau across the yellow tape, up a small hill where the security guard was sitting on a tree stump sipping on a cup of coffee.

"Pierre, the Glam cops are here to speak with you," Paperneau said, getting a chuckle out of the guard. Gray ignored the comment, figuring it to be an inside joke. He introduced himself and began asking questions about the attempted robbery.

"Do you get a lot of thefts out this way?" asked Gray.

"No, not really any point to steal this stuff before it's properly refined," replied Pierre.

"Why not?"

"Pollution, mon ami. You can't just boil this stuff and eat it. It hasn't been that way for a long time. There's a complex process that takes place to detoxify the sap before you can eat it. You would get very sick otherwise."

"Are there any other uses for the sap in its natural form?"

"Not unless you want to kill somebody."

"How much sap would you need to kill another person?"

"Depends on how it is being administered. If you put it into someone's food then you would need a pretty large amount for it to be a lethal dose. But if you put it right into their blood stream then you wouldn't need much. You could probably administer a fatal amount with a small syringe, or dipping an arrowhead or a knife in it. If not fatal, it would definitely cause a nasty infection."

"Is this common knowledge?"

"No, the industry doesn't like talking about the potential toxicity of its products. Bad for business. I'm sure they only told us because it would be against the law not to, with us working so closely to it."

Gray nodded, but felt as confused as ever. Was the perp looking to create a special weapon? Did he have knowledge of the poison or was that just a coincidence? Gray hated coincidences.

"Would someone proficient in chemistry or botany have enough working knowledge of the toxic qualities of the sap to be able to extract the poison?"

The guard shrugged his shoulders.

"How would I know? I just chase the thieves away."

"Fair enough. You told the responding officer that the van was unpainted and metal."

"Yes, that's why I thought it might be who you are looking for. I read about it in the news. The door our fuzzy Cherrie ripped off the van is leaning against one of the patrol cars."

"Did you get a good look at the thief?"

"Yeah. Guy looked crazy. He was covered in mud and sticks, bouncing around the grounds. It was like he was asking to be noticed."

"Any discernible features?"

"What, you mean like a magic twig?" Pierre asked, laughing at his own joke.

Gray stared at him, annoyed. Pierre made a coughing sound, clearing his throat. The detective's cold stare was making him uncomfortable.

"C'mon man, the guy was covered in mud. Not easy to see features. He was tall, kind of lanky. Had a bounce in his walk. Dark hair, maybe. That's about it."

Gray took down the guard's contact information and made his way back to the crime scene. Spacek was already checking out the broken van door when Gray got back inside the yellow tape.

"Looks like a match to our stolen van," said Spacek.

"Good. This should make the vehicle even easier to identify on the road," Gray replied.

"He might look to switch vehicles again once he hits the trading centre," Spacek said.

"A definite possibility, but it looks like he's lost at least some of his currency. Although I can't imagine he would have got much in return for this stuff. Find anything useful in the box?"

"No papers that will help us identify him. Mostly just sketches and notes that look like they have been written by a child."

"Let me see those."

"Be my guest; I think they're written in crayon," Spacek said as he tossed Gray the cardboard box.

Gray felt a burst of energy go through him as he rummaged through the drawings. He knew they were not from a child the moment he saw them. Although none of the notes appeared to contain any information detailing the suspect's plans, the writing was a spot-on match for the I.O.U. left at the murder scene in the car dealer's office.

"This is no child's writing, Spacek. This is from our killer. I'd bet my badge on it. We pulled a note with similar writing from the car lot scene."

Spacek nodded, but seemed to hide some surprise.

"Did you ever find similar notes in the crimes you were following in your manhunt?"

Spacek was caught off guard by the question, and took a moment to clear his throat.

"Now that you mention it, yes we did. It slipped my mind, but we did find a note written in crayon at one of the crime scenes."

Gray nodded, but wasn't convinced. Why would Spacek lie about a detail like this? Gray missed his doughnut-scarfing partner already. He felt slightly uneasy, but played it cool and decided not to push the topic any further. Gray tossed the box of notes into his trunk and thanked Paperneau for his co-operation.

"If your men can package the remaining evidence and send it to our techs in Toronto, it would be greatly appreciated," Gray said. "Oh, and send the bill for the man-hours to the TPD."

"What, you think I would have forgotten to send you the bill? This will run my guys into overtime," Sylvain replied.

"Don't worry, your men will be fully compensated for their time, Sylvain, just tell them to keep this encounter under their hats," Spacek said, chiming into the conversation.

Gray told Spacek he was going to update Gleeb on the case and began walking away from the scene towards his car. After Gray relayed the information he received from the guard to his superior, Gleeb let him know there would be a rush put on any evidence sent in.

"I'll make sure it's top priority for Diaz when it comes in," Gleeb said.

"Thanks, Captain. Crump should be back soon to speak with the reporter."

"Good thing, too. I heard she should be regaining consciousness any time now. I'm sure she'll want to see a friendly face."

"Agreed. Have there been any breaks on the assault?"

"Not really. We're hoping to learn more when Ms. Burke awakens, like why she let the perp walk through her front door."

"She let her attacker in?"

"Yeah. The guy was buzzed in from her apartment at 3:31 a.m. according to security logs, and there are no signs that her front door was forced open. He must have been someone she knew. Who else does a single woman let into her front door at that time of night?"

"Interesting. Keep me posted."

"Of course. Do you have any idea what this guy was trying to take the sap for?"

"Not sure yet, but since it has toxic qualities I think we should assume he meant to create some sort of weapon with it."

"Like a bomb?"

"No. From what one of the guards was saying, it could be used as a lethal poison if injected into the bloodstream, so I'm thinking he happened to see the farm and saw an opportunity to create a quick-and-easy weapon to use on another victim."

"Jesus. How would he even know to use this stuff?"

"I think it's safe to assume our guy has some sort of background in botany or chemistry. This stuff isn't common knowledge."

"So we're looking for an educated killer."

"I think so. I'll keep you posted, Captain."

"Thanks for the update, detective. I'll let you know if we uncover anything further on our end. Oh, and how are things going with Agent Spacek?"

"About as well as working with the F.B.I. goes," Gray replied, getting a chuckle out of his boss.

"That good, eh? Well don't worry, I'm sure this will all be over soon, and then we can fight these two clowns for who gets credit for the arrest."

"Two clowns?"

"Yeah, Spacek got the green light to join you in the manhunt from his boss, Special Agent Jacob Mincer, who has been nice enough to set himself up in one of the offices in our division. Real piece of work. I'm pretty sure this guy's suits cost as much as a week of our operating budget."

"You don't mean the whole twelve dollars, do you?"

"Very funny, detective. This guy is a bigger pain in the ass than Spacek, so get this wrapped up pronto. I want both Spacek and his boss with his stupid-looking, baby blue designer suit out of my department."

"Sure thing, Captain. We're on our way to the C.O.S.T.C.O. now. We've alerted local authorities, so they will be on the lookout for the van."

"Don't count on them, Gray. Too many locals rely on the C.O.S.T.C.O. for their goods and their livelihoods. We can't count on them when push comes to shove."

"Understood, Captain. Remember to call me with any updates if you hear anything."

"Isn't that my line, Gray?" Gleeb said with a chuckle, obviously amused by his own wit.

"Yeah, I guess it is. Talk to you soon."

One thing that always united detectives and their captains, no matter how rocky their relationship, was their dislike for the F.B.I.

"Any updates on the reporter's attacker?" Spacek asked, catching Gray off guard. Gray wondered how long Spacek had been eavesdropping on his conversation with Gleeb.

"Nothing yet," Gray replied. "Hopefully we will hear something useful once Crump has spoken with her."

"Sounds good. We should keep moving. The C.O.S.T.C.O. isn't that far from here, we can be there in two hours, one-and-a-half if we push the pedal down."

"Agreed. Let's go get this guy."

* * * *

John Crump used his lead foot to get back to Toronto for the afternoon rush hour. He put on his siren and shot through the streets taking hard turns and potholes with complete disregard for the well-being of his vehicle. It might have had something to do with the fact that the vehicle was issued to Agent Spacek and Crump didn't care for him, or the F.B.I. for that matter. When he was fresh out of the academy and policing the street, Crump always tried to please his superiors. He never minded fetching the coffee and doughnuts, or performing other menial tasks for his commanding officers. He always saw it as part of the dues you pay as a rookie and that it helped build camaraderie within a unit. But when the F.B.I. were on hand to work a case, Crump felt they treated him more like a servant than an equal. One time, an F.B.I. agent working a string of armed robberies snapped his fingers to get Crump's attention and told him to be "a good little bitch" and fetch him a cappuccino. Crump bit his tongue and brought him the coffee. The agent decided the coffee was too cold by the time Crump had brought it to him and poured it all over the rookie's shoes in front of several members of his division. Crump refrained from getting upset and said he would get him another one. The second coffee he brought back was piping hot, and Crump smiled as he watched the agent chug it down. Fifteen minutes later the agent shit his pants while attempting to run to a nearby bathroom and had to leave the scene for a change of clothes. Crump had neglected to mention to the agent that the brown sprinkles on top of the coffee were chocolate laxatives. Crump always enjoyed playing pranks, especially on people he felt deserved them or people he knew he could get a rise out of. He knew borrowing Gray's things would get him into a little hot water, but every once in a while he enjoyed moving something on his mentor's desk just for kicks. Crump figured it was his duty to lighten the guy up. He respected Gray, but felt he took trivial things far too seriously.

Our Lady of Trillium Hospital came into view as Crump got off the westbound highway. His chest tightened up as he drove closer to his destination. He was anxious to check on Monica's condition, despite resenting her a little for bruising his heart or ego — he could never figure out which one she hurt. Crump still liked her as a person and respected her abilities as a reporter. He always read the digital edition of the Gazette so he could read about Monica's latest adventures. He found her passion for the truth stimulating. That, and she had great tits — an attribute of the young reporter he constantly reminded Gray about when they saw her at crime scenes. Crump wasn't much of a smooth talker and he liked it that way. Say what you mean, and mean what you say. That's what he believed.

After spending ten minutes circling the parking lot, he found a spot to park and walked inside through the emergency room entrance. It looked like a pretty calm day in paradise. Only a few people waiting to be treated and no one appeared to be bleeding out of their ears. He flashed his badge at the main desk and asked a short, podgy black woman in candy stripes for Monica's room number.

"Hey there, sugar," the woman said in a cheerful tone. "You're in luck, she just woke up."

Crump was filled with relief and joy.

"That's fantastic! Where is she?"

"Whoa, cowboy, you've got to take it easy on her. She's been through a lot. Try not to raise her stress level too much."

Crump nodded in agreement, and then checked his hair in the reflection of a glass-framed painting that hung on the wall behind the nurse. It was a picture of a man and a woman walking down a dock. The painted couple was sharing a bag of fries from a fry stand.

"So this visit — is it business or personal?" the nurse asked, apparently teasing the young detective.

"Both," he replied while grinning. "By the way, I like your painting."

"Thanks, it was done by an artist in New Quebec. Apparently he painted it from a photo he snapped of a place called Campbellton."

"Cool. Looks like they have good fries. So what's the room number?"

"Room 218. But remember, take it easy on her."

"Not a problem, honey. I'm always easy on the ladies," he said as he winked at the nurse.

"I'm sure you are," the nurse said while smiling back.

When Crump got to Monica's room, he was surprised to see that she didn't have any visitors. It had only been a few days since the attack, so it seemed strange not to have anyone around offering their support. Monica's eyes turned to Crump as he entered the room. She smiled for a moment when she saw him, making him grin like an idiot. She quickly changed to a serious demeanour and Crump did the same.

"Detective Crump, if you're here to take my statement you're a little late. Another officer has already done that."

"That's okay, Monica. I just wanted to make sure you were alright. How are you feeling?"

"Like I just got robbed, beaten and left for dead in my own home by a pizza delivery man."

Crump grabbed a chair and sat down next to her. "Did the bastard try anything else?" he whispered.

"No, the asshole didn't try to rape me if that's what you mean. I guess I should be thankful for that."

Crump breathed a small sigh of relief.

"You getting soft on me detective? Or should I say, soft again?" the reporter asked while letting out a painful laugh.

"Oh fuck you, Monica. I just drank too much that night. I told you that already," Crump responded as he felt his face blush. He would have been angrier, but she had a playful smile on her face when she said it that made the comment feel more like a sadistic form of flirting than a shot at his manliness. Crump loved her smart ass attitude.

He asked Monica if she could go through the events leading up to the night of the attack one more time for him, to see if he might be able to generate a lead. She told him about the connection she found in the photos and the message she left for Gray. Crump took out his smartphone and began skimming through his photo album.

"You know that's supposed to be turned off in the hospital, detective," she said, continuing to tease him. Crump smiled in response.

"C'mon now, darling, how can anything be turned off around you?"

He could see Monica blush underneath her bruises as she smiled back. Crump enlarged his photo of Spacek on his phone and showed it to her.

"Does this guy look familiar at all?"

Monica stared at the image for a few moments before responding.

"Not really. Sorry. Is he a suspect?"

"No, just an asshole," Crump said as he put away his phone.

Monica was instantly interested in the man in the photo.

"That's the talk of interagency co-operation," she said.

"Ha! You nailed that one, I'll give you that. But no more — I can't talk about this case. Anyway, you should get some rest."

"Fuck that noise, rookie. I want to catch this guy."

Crump couldn't stop smiling at the sassy reporter.

"You up for seeing a sketch artist so we can try and I.D. this prick?"

"I'm always up for grabbing a prick. You should know that by now," she said while winking.

Crump smiled as he dialed the number of his precinct.

"Alright then, let's get sketching."

9

DIRTY DEALINGS

By the time I made my way back up the hill, my clothes were dry and I could hear a dinner bell being rung somewhere within the trading centre. The sky was a lovely chestnut-tangerine. It reminded me of the many sunsets Rose and I would watch at the start of a long night of drinking. The merchants had lit torches all along the path leading back to the central trading area in preparation for sunset. I walked the path slowly so I could take the time to admire all that Mother Nature had to offer. I could not comprehend how a place so beautiful could remain so close to being completely untainted by the plague of humanity's so-called progress. As I walked the path I noticed a large cloud of black smoke filling the sky in the distance. It appeared to be coming from the direction of the road I travelled on to get into the C.O.S.T.C.O.

Oh cruel fate! How could you throw such a twisted tool of the monkeys into my plans? As quickly as I had questioned the actions of fate, it replied in the form of a young couple walking past me hand-in-hand, discussing the smoking phenomena. The man on the left wore glasses, had bronze-coloured skin and a powerful afro. He had thick sideburns that ran down his cheeks and connected to his moustache. He wore a gold chain that bounced against the exposed chest hair that protruded from his half-buttoned, tan-coloured shirt. The man's other half wore similar eyewear, but the top of his head shined from the glare of the torches as he walked, allowing any passerby to stare at the full beauty of his bald-eagle dome. His moustache gave him the look of a B-movie porn star. He looked greasy. His moustache could not be trusted. His grey shirt and maroon-coloured tie gave him the appearance of a sneaky salesman. Or perhaps it was his moustache? I suppose it didn't really matter.

"Did you hear about the road being closed due to a forest fire, honeybunch?" the bronzed man asked his significant other.

"Shut up, fool! Don't make me give you a little more of this!" the man's balding half replied as he quickly snatched his hand away from his partner and raised the back of it in his lover's direction. "Who cares about the forest fire? It was probably some careless jerkoff smoking cigarettes where they shouldn't be. All I care about is getting your ass into the kitchen so you can make my dinner."

The man with the untrustworthy moustache then playfully smacked the bronze man's behind.

His partner giggled in response to his boyfriend's gesture. "I guess you're right as always, peaches. Let's get home, so I can bake you a pie."

The couple walked by me without saying another word. They looked truly content. So few of us get to experience that feeling of completeness with another human being. It made me miss Rose. I couldn't believe someone could have potentially started a forest fire with an errantly thrown cigarette. Some people are so careless. I just hoped someone else's stupidity wouldn't delay my trip back into Glamerica. I was running short on time as it was. When I arrived at the main trading area, Jeremiah was sitting at his tent slinging back a large tin mug of frothy brew.

"Well look at what the cat dragged in," he said while looking in my direction. "Mister, I gots some good news, and I gots some bad news. What do you want first?"

A lump built up in my throat at the thought of my journey ending here, spending my last precious days alone at the C.O.S.T.C.O., or worse yet, with Jeremiah working off the cost of his labour. I took a deep breath and asked for the bad news first.

"The bad news is your van is fucked. It's leaked almost all of its fluids, and with all the damage it has sustained, it ain't driveable. It wouldn't have got you more than a few clicks up the road before givin' up the ghost at this point."

My heart dropped into my stomach. Was my mission truly over? Jeremiah interrupted my thoughts of failure.

"Now don't be giving Jeremiah them sad eyes and pouty lips. There somewhere you needed to be?"

"Mississauga. More than I've ever needed to be somewhere in my entire life."

The old grease monkey lifted up his ballcap and gave his head a scratch. He could see the look of desperation on my face and it appeared to make him uncomfortable.

"Well, I tell you what, there are still some good working parts on this van that I could salvage for a few bucks. So if you're in a hurry to hit the road I can trade you ol' Gladis in exchange for your vehicle," he said as he removed the dust cover off an old orange motorcycle. "Ol' Gladis doesn't move like she used to so I wouldn't ride her on the big highways. But she's a two-stroke, so she will still do you right along the back roads and rural highways. With the main road blocked off due to the forest fire, she might be your best bet for gettin' where you need to get. I can even make you a map of the back roads out of here towards ol' T.O."

"Done!" I yelled as I ran over to Jeremiah and gave him a hug. The old man blushed as he handed me the key to the bike.

My heart was pounding. My mission wasn't over! I hopped onto the bike and turned the key. The engine wheezed for a moment, but started, creating a loud humming sound and gently vibrating my seat.

"I tossed your things from the van into an old backpack," Jeremiah said as he handed me the bag. "I even added a few things to keep your motor running on your journey."

I slung the bag over my shoulders and dusted off an old helmet to wear as the mechanic drew me up a rough map of the area. He even wrote down directions of the best paths to take to get home. I thanked Jeremiah for his help, then peeled out of his lot. As I drove out of the central trading area towards an old path leading back to Glamerica, I passed by Kailey, who was sleeping peacefully in a hammock. I decided I couldn't leave without saying goodbye, especially after all we had been through. I stopped the bike, put it into reverse and slowly backed it into Kailey's lot. I stopped about eight feet from the hammock. I couldn't help but ogle the red-haired beauty for a few moments before saying goodbye. She was wearing black pajama bottoms and her plaid jacket, which was unbuttoned, exposing her white crop top, which rode up her stomach enough to show off her impressive abs. She wore no bra, allowing me a glimpse of her puffy nipples, which looked like they were trying to push their way out of her shirt. I thought about the best way to say goodbye. It took me about a minute, minus the fifty-six seconds I spent staring at Kailey's nipples. I slammed on the horn as I put the bike into drive and punched the gas. Startled by the noise, the red-headed warrior fell out of her hammock on to the ground making a thump sound. It would have been a clean getaway if it wasn't for the mud underneath my tires. The bike's rear tire fired a barrage of muddy projectiles into Kailey's lot before I was able to speed off.

As I made my way out of the C.O.S.T.C.O., I was stopped by a man driving a blue sedan. He was dressed casually in a pair of ripped blue jeans and a heavy metal t-shirt, but he wore a stern look. He appeared to mean business, whatever business that might be. He had another man with him that made me more uncomfortable. He stared intensely at me. He had a ghostly look on his face, like he just got caught with his hand in the cookie jar.

"Hey, buddy, we're looking to buy a used van. Know of any up for grabs?" asked the man in the heavy metal t-shirt.

"Actually, there might be one available at Lot 23. It's a ten-minute drive down the main path," I replied.

"What's it look like?"

"It's silver or grey. But don't get your hopes up. The van looks fucked. Probably wouldn't get you more than a few clicks before givin' up the ghost. Might be okay for parts, though."

"Sounds like just the kind of vehicle we're looking for. Thanks, pal," the heavy metal fan said as he and his friend drove down the path.

The two men were in such a hurry they almost hit the tall, mud-covered figure that was running up the path shouting obscenities. How cute, she misses me already, I thought as I drove onto a dirt path and began my journey home.

10

GOD DAMN WOLVES!

My return trip home went smoothly for the first twenty kilometres of windy back roads. Jeremiah's map turned out to be pretty reliable, despite being written on a greasy napkin by a man whose writing could have gotten him mistaken for a medical professional. As I drove through the dense foliage of the forest, my bike began to sputter and slow down. I cursed my negotiating skills as I realized I hadn't asked Jeremiah to toss in a full tank of gas. Things began to look hopeless as I coasted to a stop by a small dirt path that led to an old cottage. The home looked abandoned, but I was desperate, so I leaned my bike against a tree, lit up a smoke and walked down the path. The smell of pine refreshed and calmed my spirits as I made my way to the home. The scent was helpful for keeping me calm, since the weathered cottage looked like something out of a slasher film the closer I got. The stone base was covered in chips and cracks. Some areas were completely covered in moss. The wood that made up the majority of the walls was covered in peeling paint and rot. There were undefinable spatter-like stains covering various sections of the walls and a white picket fence surrounding a small collection of crops. The tops of carrots poked out of the dirt next to at least a dozen corn stalks that stood eight feet tall. Walking around the home towards the front door I tried to peer into the windows to see if anyone was home, but all the windows on the first floor were boarded up. When I got to the front door, I walked up three steps that creaked loudly. They sank slightly each step I took. It felt like I could fall through them at any moment. I felt relieved as I made my way past the final step and walked towards the large wooden double doors. It was almost eight o'clock at night so I hoped someone, preferably not a serial killer, had already called it a day and was relaxing inside. There was no doorbell so I rapped my knuckles hard against one of the red doors. Paint from the door transferred to my knuckles. It was fresh. I took that as a positive sign that the home was still inhabited. I prayed someone would answer — and by pray I mean I crossed my fingers really hard — despite the fact that the homeowner might be a reclusive cannibal. I've never thought it wise to walk the properties of backwoods country folk. They are often extremely distrustful of outsiders, and have been known to attack trespassers on sight. The faint sound of rumblings coming from inside the house made me jump and my heart race with anticipation and fear. I took a couple of steps back and put on my most welcoming smile in the hope of making a good first impression. While I waited for someone to open the door, I surveyed the damage done by my door knocking. I hoped they wouldn't be too upset that I ruined their paint job. Upon close inspection, I could see cracks running throughout both doors' entire structures. They appeared to have been completely destroyed at some point and then put back together and repainted.

Was this home the victim of an overly aggressive travelling salesman desperate to make a sale? Or perhaps a raid? Was this place once a grow-op? Is it a grow-op now? Are their rates reasonable?

All sorts of questions raced through my mind as the rumbling from within grew exponentially louder. The sounds felt like they were getting closer in a hurry. Big, fluffy doggy?

The creature burst through the doors, sending splinters of wood in every direction. It swept me off my feet and drove me off the porch. It was not a big, fluffy doggy. I gripped on to the front of the monster to try and avoid being steamrolled into the dirt path. My eyes would never have opened to see my attacker if it were not for the war cry that followed the surprise assault.

"Game on!" a crackly male voice yelled.

I opened my eyes and realized my arms and legs were wrapped around a turbo-charged Zamboni being driven by a cackling old man in a blue hockey helmet, a stained white undershirt, blue shorts and red sandals. The old man spun the steering wheel with vigor, although it did not appear to have any effect on the direction the vehicle took. I turned my head to see where the deranged shut-in was taking me and stared in horror as we headed towards a padded barrier that stood only a few feet above the ground. Beyond the barrier laid a large pen, populated with pink, podgy creatures of the pork variety. I pulled myself to the top of the Zamboni in a mad scramble to avoid getting crushed. When the ice grooming machine impacted with the barrier it sent me hurdling into the pigpen. I shot across the pen sending tidal waves of mud in every direction. I screamed shortly before colliding with a plump pork product that squealed frantically. The two of us held each other tightly as we braced for impact. We bowled over a handful of the pig's pen pals, sending them into the air in a manner that would mystify those that once doubted the creatures' abilities to take to the skies. The two of us continued to sail through the pen until we connected with the feeding trough. Within the blink of an eye, my fear had dissipated from my body and everything was dark…

"Wake up, Remy! It's Christmas and I want to open the presents!" Rose said as she hovered over me, bouncing up and down on my mattress.

Her emerald eyes glowed beyond their natural beauty this morning. She had the anticipation and energy of a child.

"C'mon! C'mon! C'mon! Move it, lazy bum!" She said as she grabbed hold of the bed sheet underneath my slumbering carcass and tugged, flinging me onto the floor.

"I guess I don't need all my bones to be intact to celebrate Christmas," I said as I laid face down, buck naked, kissing a creaky wooden floorboard.

"Nah, not after you see what I got you, pasty buns," Rose responded while hopping on to my back and spanking my bottom repeatedly, making loud smack sounds.

She always knew how to get me out of bed on my days off, which was helpful since most days were days off.

"Enough already — we'll open the damn gifts!" I said.

I always submitted to Rose's will on Christmas. I suppose it was because I knew how important the holiday was to her.

"Thanks, baby. I'll go put on some coffee," she said as she leaned down and pressed her gentle lips against my cheek.

Rose then hopped to her feet and ran to the kitchen.

I grabbed hold of the mattress and pulled myself to my feet. After slipping into my favourite pair of fleece pyjama pants to protect my abused bottom from future spankings, I made my way to the kitchen for my morning coffee. Stumbling half-asleep into the kitchen, I wrapped my arms around Rose from behind. One of my favourite physical characteristics of Rose was her petite frame. I loved being able to engulf her entire body with a hug. When she was wrapped tightly in my arms, it felt like none of the negative elements in this world could ever affect us. As long as I was holding her, the world as I knew it could come to an end and I would die a happy man. Rose wrapped her delicate arms around mine and gazed up at me.

"Merry Christmas, Remy. I love you."

"I love you too, Rose."

I stroked her short, raven black hair, tilted her head back and placed my lips on hers. They felt like leather and tasted like goat milk. Weird.

"Breathe, damn you!" an unfamiliar voice yelled.

This time I awoke to the touch of the cracked, dry lips of a crazed old man in a hockey helmet. I attempted to jump to my feet but kept slipping due to the mud inside the pigpen where I had laid unconscious for an unknown period of time. I flopped around like a fish, splashing mud everywhere.

"Calm down there, kid. You weren't breathin' right so I was helping you steer clear of the bright light," the old man said.

I grabbed hold of a section of fence in the pigpen for balance and pulled myself to my feet.

"Christ, what the hell happened?" I asked.

"Sorry about the surprise greeting there, kiddo. I thought you were a wolf looking to steal my crops."

"But I knocked on the door."

"So do the wolves, kid."

The crazy old bastard had obviously been out in the woods too long. Too much time in isolation can play with a person's mind. I hoped he still knew what gasoline was.

"Okay then. Well, the reason I knocked on your door is because my bike ran out of gas and I was wondering if you could spare a little so I could get home."

The old man looked surprised.

"Well shit, sonny. If that's all you wanted, why didn't you just say so? You don't need to go rummaging through a man's pigpen for that."

"Huh?"

"You young people need to learn to respect people's property better. I'll get you a small canister, but I expect two new doors to come in the mail."

"What?"

"The doors you broke. You owe me two new ones."

"Uh, sure thing, grandpa. I'll get you more doors."

"Well then, we're good. By the way, I'm Eli."

"Remy. Good to meet you. I just came from the C.O.S.T.C.O."

The old man shook his head in disapproval.

"That's a wicked place, son. I'll pray you get out of there soon."

"I'm actually on my way home. I need to get there before the world ends."

"No problem, son. Let me go get you some gas."

I followed Eli as he made his way back to his home. I tried to read my map to check my route, but the mud had destroyed it.

"Hey, could you give me directions around the forest fire a few kilometres south of here? I need to get back home to Mississauga."

"Sure, kid. There's a trail behind my place that should take you around the fire and back onto the closest highway, the NQ-105. Take it south to the NQ-301. It should only take you a few hours until you come across a small bridge that will bring you back into Ontario. It will save a ton of time compared to taking the other back roads around here. It's a shame that fire broke out in the forest. Those trees are real old, practically ancient. The authorities are going to be looking for blood."

"As they should," I replied. "People need to learn to be less careless. This forest is part of people's homes."

"You don't have to tell me, kid. Just wait here and I'll be back in a minute with your gas."

Eli kicked a few door splinters aside as he entered his home. My stomach began to rumble and gurgle as I waited for the old man to return. While admiring Eli's garden I realized I couldn't remember the last time I ate. I walked over to his garden and peered over the wooden fence to search for potential snacks. I reached over the fence and yanked a plump carrot out of the ground. While brushing the dirt off it a shotgun blast barely missed cutting me in half. The buckshot hit the corn stalks beside me, sending cob and kernels everywhere.

"Wolves!" Eli yelled while preparing to reload his gun.

Jesus, I didn't even hear them coming! I screamed in fear for my life and ran towards Eli for protection. As I ran towards his porch my right foot partially broke through the third step sending me stumbling into the old man, knocking us both to the ground. I jumped to my feet and turned towards the forest to see where the wolves were coming from, but couldn't identify the source of the old man's panic. Eli was rolling from side to side in pain, making groaning and gurgling sounds. I knelt down to help him to his feet, but the old man was bleeding everywhere. The carrot I grabbed was now protruding from his abdomen. I had no idea you could stab someone with a carrot.

"God damn wolves!" he muttered at me before losing consciousness.

The poor old bastard must have been hallucinating. It's a shame that some people live out their lives alone in this kind of isolation. It eats away at your sanity. He's probably going to a better place now. Beside Eli's body was a red plastic container. I picked it up and the fluid inside sloshed back and forth.

"Sweet nectar!" I yelled as I made my way back down the path where Gladis sat, awaiting more gassy goodness.

After refuelling my bike, I grabbed a few carrots for the long journey ahead. Hopefully I won't have to use them. I hate violence. I slipped the carrots into my pack and began my drive through the trail behind Eli's home.

* * * *

Gray and Spacek sped through the trading centre, in a mad
scramble to find Lot 23. Spacek gripped onto the holy-shit
handle for dear life as his partner took sharp turns on the narrow
dirt paths that comprised most of the roads. Gray slowed the
car down and parked on the side of the road when he noticed a
beat up van matching the suspect's vehicle sitting in plain sight
on a trading lot about 50 feet in front of him. Jeremiah had his
head deep in the van's hood.

"What's the plan, detective?" Spacek said as he took off his seatbelt. He appeared a little rattled. Gray picked up on his nervousness immediately.

"The behemoth hillbilly doesn't match the description of our perp, for what good the description we have is. This place appears to be some sort of repair shop. We should sit tight and grab him when he comes back for his vehicle."

"Are you nuts? We need to question this guy now," Spacek replied as he exited the vehicle and began a fast-paced walk towards the super-sized mechanic.

Gray wanted to question the man as well, but wanted to see how Spacek would react. He could tell something was off with his new partner ever since they entered the C.O.S.T.C.O. Gray exited the car and followed Spacek to Lot 23. The F.B.I. agent flashed his badge to Jeremiah and the big man scratched his head.

"Ain't you fellas in the wrong country?" he asked.

"This country only exists because my government allows it to exist," Spacek replied.

"Well, in that case, go fuck yourself," Jeremiah said, as he turned his attention back towards the hood of the van.

Spacek grabbed Jeremiah by his arm. The big man reacted immediately, shoving the agent on to the ground. Jeremiah then picked up a large pipe wrench and raised it in the air in a threatening manner towards Spacek. The agent pulled his service pistol and was ready to fire, but Gray jumped in between them, motioning for both men to lower their weapons.

"Sir, we're hunting a dangerous man, and we believe this was his vehicle," Gray said, quickly diffusing the volatile situation. "The man we're looking for has already killed at least two people, maybe more. We need your co-operation. What can you tell me about the man who brought this van to you?"

Jemeriah lowered his wrench, while keeping his eyes focused on agent Spacek, who slowly holstered his gun.

"All I can tell you is, whoever you're looking for ain't the guy that brought me this van," Jeremiah said. "This fella was harmless, although a tad too stressed if you ask me."

"What do you mean?" Gray replied.

"This fella was in a hell of a hurry to get to Mississauga. Needed to get there, and I quote, 'More than I've ever needed to be somewhere in my entire life.' Must be something real important down that way."

"Do you know what he was doing in the C.O.S.T.C.O.?" Gray asked.

"Trading, like everyone else," Jeremiah replied, as he lowered his voice. "I saw him chattin' with the Carbonneau clan a little while ago. Them folks have been known to sell the odd heavy weapon and explosive ordinance, but you didn't hear that from me."

Spacek and Gray looked at each other.

"You can search the van if that helps," Jeremiah said, walking around to the back of the van.

"I'll call HQ and give them an update," Spacek said.

Gray nodded and followed Jeremiah to the back of the vehicle. The back of the mechanic's lot was encumbered with piles of random junk. It looked like a poorly organized scrap yard. The two men hopped inside the back of the van, so Gray could inspect the area.

"Do you know where the man is now?" Gray asked.

"I traded him ol' Gladis for his van, straight up."

Gray gave Jeremiah a puzzled look.

"Ol' Gladis?"

"My orange motorcycle. I may have oversold the damage on this here vehicle to him, but I still think it was a fair trade."

Gray's eyes lit up.

"Son of a bit–"

All of a sudden Gray felt the paralyzing sting of a Taser shocking his body into unconsciousness. The detective crumpled on to the floor of the van. Jeremiah stood frozen for a moment, as he looked down the silenced barrel of Spacek's pistol. Then everything in Jeremiah's mind went dark. Gray and Jeremiah laid together in a heap on the floor of the van. Spacek holstered his weapons and pulled out his cell phone from his jacket. He made a call as he grabbed an old dust cover and threw it over the gaping hole at the back of the van. Spacek grabbed some duct tape and began attaching the dust cover to the vehicle, as the man on the other end of the agent's phone call picked up.

"Our target is headed home," said Spacek.

"Excellent. And the detective?"

"Unconscious in the suspect's vehicle, inside the C.O.S.T.C.O. How would you like me to proceed?"

"Drive it out of the trading centre, and light it up."

"With or without the detective inside?"

"Do you think he'll be a problem for us?"

"Maybe."

"Then let him go up in smoke."

11

G'DAY FROM THE VALLEY

The path around the rancher's home was surrounded by dense foliage and towering pines. After a few rights and lefts I completely lost my sense of direction. Navigating the winding road reminded me of old tales of minotaurs and their labyrinths. Unsuspecting treasure hunters would find themselves lost in the man-beasts' homes shortly before falling victim to them. Luckily for me those creatures are make-believe, although my ribs were beginning to feel as if a minotaur's horns had been driven right through them. God damn wolves!

After a few hours of driving I was able to cover some solid ground. I followed Eli's directions and shot down the NQ-105 South, over to the NQ-301 South, and drove until I came to a small wooden bridge that took me across the Ottawa River into Ontario. I hopped onto Highway 17 and followed it until it brought me to the town of Arnprior.

I spotted a gas station with a fry truck in its lot and stopped for a quick fill-up and a bite. The fry truck had a big wooden sign nailed to the top that said "Packer's Place," right below the serving window. A man in his forties leaned against the window from inside the truck. He used his elbow as a stand so his hand could hold up his chin. He looked very bored. The glaze over the man's eyes began to clear as I approached his truck. He stood up at attention, ready to make a few bucks from a passerby. He brushed off his greasy apron and straightened his Redmen ballcap in preparation to take my order.

"Well g'day from the Valley, stranger. Welcome to Packer's. How many fries can Jason pack away for ya?" the man asked.

"Are your fries any good?"

"Best in the Valley," Jason replied.

"That's what the sign said in Renfrew."

"Don't trust 'em. Lying bastards, all of 'em. It's a good thing you stopped here and not at Renfrew's fry shack. If you did, you'd be sharting for a week."

I nodded in response. I always felt I could trust a man who was willing to use words like shart.

"Okay, Jason, one Packer's special."

"You got it," Jason said as he proceeded to toss fries into the fryer.

"What do you have to drink?" I asked.

"Diet cola."

"Do you have anything else?"

"Why would I have anything else?"

"Uh, never mind. One diet cola."

Jason tossed a can of diet soda out of his serving window into my waiting hands. I popped it open and took a few sips while I waited for my fries. Diet soda tastes like ass, but I was thirsty.

"If you have some free time you should head downtown and check out what our town has to offer. We used to be a small rural community, before all the development came in and turned us into a big city," Jason said.

I turned my head left and right, noticing a few small developments outside of the town's downtown core. They appeared to be surrounded by farmers' fields.

"What's the population of this town? Like three hundred?" I asked.

Jason raised his right eyebrow before responding. It was a menacing-looking eyebrow.

"Let me guess — you're from Toronto."

"Mississauga. How did you know?"

"Just a hunch. I'll make sure to give you the Toronto discount."

"Thanks! How much do I owe you?"

"Twelve bucks."

"But the sign says ten dollars."

"Yup. Twelve bucks, please."

I decided not to argue and paid Jason out of the last eighty dollars of Sal's petty cash.

"So, what brings you to Arnprior?"

"Just passing through."

"You sure you won't stay awhile and check out the sites?"

"Thanks, but I can't," I said as I grabbed the bag of fries. "The end of the world is coming and I need to get home."

Jason stared at me. He looked annoyed.

"And people wonder why I'm getting so curmudgeonly in my old age. Bloody nutcases," he said. "Congratulations, you just tasted the best fries in the Valley. Now get out of here before I slap a figure-four leg lock on ya!"

Knowing full well the devastation of the figure-four, I ran to my bike, shovelling fries down my gullet the entire time. They were delicious! I hopped on Ol' Gladis and drove through the town until I hit Highway 29 and went south, following the Mississippi River through the town of Almonte and into Carleton Place. The drive was fun and relaxing. I always enjoyed drives on rural roads. They were much more enjoyable than dodging truck traffic on the ever-busy Highway 401. After turning west onto Highway 7, I stopped at a local 24-hour cheese shop. It looked like it had been there for a while. Most of Carleton Place was comprised of big-box outlet stores and sprawling suburban communities, but this one store appeared to stand the test of time. I parked my bike and went inside. The smell of various cheeses filled my nostrils instantly. I grabbed a small package of fresh cheddar cheese, a box of crackers and a half-pound of homemade fudge, and then walked over to the cashier.

"Will that be everything today?" asked the older woman at the cash, while giving me a warm and welcoming smile.

"Yeah, this should do it," I replied. "By the way, why is this town called Carleton Place?"

"Because the Carleton family owns it," she replied.

"Who's Carleton?"

"Some old, rich Scottish guy. He owns some famous square overseas."

"Oh. Does he own any famous circles or triangles?"

"Uh, not that I know of."

"Pfft, just one measly square? Anyone can own one of those."

"Well I'm sorry our town's history doesn't impress you, sir," the woman said in a less sunny tone. "Let me guess, you're just passing through on your way back home to Toronto."

"Mississauga. Wow, you valley folk are like mind readers."

"It's our special gift."

"Cool. Well, thanks for the history lesson. See ya!" I said as I quickly walked out the door in an effort to avoid another Toronto discount.

I stuffed a pile of crackers into my mouth and bit a chunk of cheese off my block of cheddar as I hopped onto my bike and took off towards home.

My drive lasted about thirty minutes before I noticed the needle on my gas tank pointing towards empty. My fear of the figure-four had made me forget to fill up when I grabbed my fries. Fortunately, I spotted a sign for a gas station as I made my way into the town of Perth. As I entered the town's borders I passed a sign that read "Perth, Glamerica's home for history buffs." I figured the town was packed full of people well-versed in the history of Glamerica and the local area. It'll be a shame when all that knowledge is burned up in a nuclear blaze.

When I pulled into the gas station I was greeted by an elderly man in a green trucker's cap, and nothing else. He was standing at attention by the pumps in his birthday suit, and it wasn't a cause for celebration.

"Welcome to Perth, young man. Can I fill you up?" the attendant asked.

"Not with that thing. Must be colder than I thought for a night in July," I replied. "But you can top up my bike."

The attendant burst out laughing, making his jingly parts jiggle.

"Hey, it's midnight and the mosquitos are hungry. What do you want me to do, give them a bigger target? That would be reckless. You must not be from around here."

"Nope, I'm from… er… so, why are you naked?" I asked.

"You're in Perth, home of Glamerica's greatest historians and the only five-star nudist colony in the country."

"Seems like an odd mix."

"Not really. We historians love to know our stuff in the buff."

"How are the winters?"

"They're hell, but at least they kill these damn mosquitos. You can't have everything, am I right?"

"I guess. How long has this town been a nudist colony?"

"Ever since the manufacturing left. As a town we were shifting ourselves towards becoming a retirement community anyways, so the nudist colony theme just seemed like it would fit in nicely."

"How do you figure?"

"Have you ever been to a nude beach, son? There's rarely anyone under the age of sixty-five. And we elderly love our museums; they celebrate the highs and lows of the past. Our pasts included."

"So you're telling me this town is a collection of museums and naked old people?"

"You got it."

"Um, is my bike full yet? I'd really like to keep moving."

The elderly man rolled his eyes at me.

"Prude. Yeah, yeah, your tank is full. That'll be thirty-two bucks."

"Really? That seems cheap — not that I'm complaining."

"Government subsidies, sonny. Having the only five-star nudist colony has its benefits. We're a very popular retirement spot for government employees, and they take care of their own."

I nodded politely, pretending to understand the relationship as I hopped back onto my motorcycle and drove out of Perth. Thoughts of Rose and an end to my quest began to fill my mind as I continued my drive down Highway 7 towards home.

* * * *

Gray awoke to his body bouncing inside the back of the van, due to Spacek's inability to miss the potholes on the backwoods roads. Gray had a massive headache and the muscles in his neck were sore and stiff, but he felt okay, otherwise. His hands were cuffed behind his back to a piece of the van's mangled frame. Spacek appeared to be concentrating on trying to navigate the roads, so he didn't notice Gray wriggling around on the floor, attempting to get his left hand into the back pocket of his blue jeans. Gray always liked to keep a spare key to his handcuffs on him, in case a perp ever got the jump on him and used his cuffs against him. It was a practice he used ever since an embarrassing incident involving a female perp.

With only four months on the job, Gray stumbled upon Lydia LeBrecque, a well-known cat burglar, while investigating a tripped alarm at a luxury apartment in downtown Toronto. He attempted to catch her in the act before backup arrived, and was tasered and handcuffed with his own cuffs to a radiator for his trouble. Tasers still carry an extra sting for Gray, which made him even more pissed off at Spacek.

Gray pulled the spare key from his pocket but it slipped from his fingertips as the van slowed down and came to an abrupt halt. The key slid into the pool of blood that had oozed out of Jeremiah's head wound and formed a large puddle around Gray's feet. The detective dragged the key out of the blood with his foot and went to work on the handcuffs.

Spacek hopped out of the van, holding Gray's service weapon in his right hand. The F.B.I. agent breathed deeply and let the scent of fresh pine enter his nostrils as he walked around to the back doors of the vehicle to complete his mission. Spacek had parked the van down a remote dirt road that led to an old cottage. It appeared abandoned, but in the distance, Spacek thought he saw a small crop of corn behind a white picket fence. It was difficult to see in the thick of the night.

Creepy. Spacek thought to himself as opened the back door to the van.

Gray was lying motionless on the floor, his shoes and pants covered in blood.

"Wake up, detective," Spacek said while kicking the bottom of Gray's shoes. "It's time to punch out."

"If you say so," Gray replied as he mule kicked Spacek in the groin.

Spacek stumbled backwards a few steps, giving Gray a chance to get to his feet. Gray lunged forward at Spacek, attempting to land a haymaker with his handcuff-wrapped left hand. The blood on the soles of Gray's shoes caused him to lose his balance just enough to turn his knockout punch into a glancing blow that cut open the agent's chin. Gray landed roughly onto the dirt road as Spacek let out a painful cry. The F.B.I. agent had his gun pointed at Gray's head before he had a chance to mount another attack.

"You nosy fuck," Spacek screamed. "You should have handed this case over to us when you had the chance."

"Why the hell are this perp's crimes so important to you?" Gray replied, trying to make sense of Spacek's actions.

"Ha! We couldn't give a shit about his crimes."

"Then why run all over the place chasing him?"

"That's above both our pay grades. I'm just paid to bring Mr. Delemme in."

"You son of a bitch, you knew who this guy was all along?"

"Ever since the maple farm. Mr. Delemme failed to remove his identification from the desk that fell out of his vehicle and splintered all over the road. It appears the perp that's been so good at eluding you really wasn't that stealthy after all."

"Maybe that was never his game," Gray said in response, although he was talking more to himself than with the agent of his impending destruction.

Spacek laughed as he shook his head at the detective.

"Tobias Gray, the hunter of Toronto's most devious offenders, can't convince himself he simply got outplayed by a killer. We all lose a step at some point, detective. Your misstep just happened to cost you your life," Spacek replied as he took aim at Gray with the detective's own service pistol.

"One last question," Gray said.

"Shoot," Spacek replied with a sadistic smile.

"If you knew who he was at the C.O.S.T.C.O., why didn't you just grab him then?"

"Too many witnesses. That, and it will be easier to grab him with you off my back. My team is pinpointing his destination as we speak. We'll nab him once he feels safe and secure. Less chance of casualties that way. After all, we are dealing with a dangerous killer. I mean, just look at what he did to the poor soul in the van, and what he's about to do to one of TPD's finest. Goodbye, detective Gr—"

Spacek's final sentence was cut short when a shotgun blast struck his back and opened up his chest, spraying blood into Gray's face. Spacek's body collapsed in a heap at Gray's feet. Gray was now looking down the barrel of a much bigger, smoking gun. At the end of the barrel was an old man dressed in blue shorts, a blood-stained undershirt, red sandals and a hockey helmet. He appeared to be suffering from a wound in his abdomen. Gray sat frozen, awaiting a response from the man who could just as easily be his saviour or his executioner.

"God damn wolves! Did he bite you?" The man asked as he reloaded his shotgun.

"No. Thanks for your help," Gray replied.

"Don't thank me yet, sonny. Who are you and what are you doing on my land?" the old man asked as he pointed the barrel of his gun at the detective.

Gray raised his hand in a gesture of peace, hoping the old man would lower his weapon.

"Don't shoot. I'm detective Tobias Gray of the Toronto Police Department."

The old man breathed a sigh of relief and lowered his weapon.

"Well, took you guys long enough. How many times does an old man have to complain about wolves attacking his crops before you government types get off your asses and do something about it?"

Gray stared back with no response. He was still worried about making any sudden movements and spooking the old man.

"Well, at least you're here now," the man said. "Let me help you up and take a look at ya."

The old man outstretched his arm to Gray and helped pull him to his feet. Gray pulled his t-shirt up and rubbed Spacek's blood off his face. He noticed the old man's wound appeared to still be bleeding.

"Sir, what's your name?"

"Eli."

"Well, Eli, I appreciate your help. That, um, wolf, was going to take my life. I owe you one. Why don't you let me repay you by checking that wound in your gut."

Eli nodded and lifted his shirt, exposing a bloody rag held onto his stomach with a couple pieces of duct tape.

"God damn wolf got me, officer. Never saw it coming, neither. Got me with my own carrot," Eli explained while pointing to the crops behind the white picket fence.

"I think I can patch this up for now with the right supplies, but you'll need to see a doctor and get some stitches," Gray replied.

"No need, I got staples."

"If you say so, Eli. Do you have a first-aid kit?"

"Pfft. You see the duct tape, don't ya? Besides, aren't you guys given any supplies? I can't just be tossing around my duct tape to every would-be doctor that comes strollin' on to my land," Eli said as he lowered his shirt, apparently no longer interested in Gray's offer to help patch him up. Gray chose his next words carefully, knowing full well he was dealing with a man that had serious mental health issues. The detective knew not to provoke men like Eli. He had seen the horrors that can stem from a negotiator saying the wrong thing at the wrong time too many times. He had been that negotiator.

"Fair enough, Eli. Do you have a phone I can use?"

"Nope, it's been dead for years."

"Then how have you been calling to complain about the wolves?"

"Who said I was calling anyone?"

"Never mind, Eli. The wolf that got you, what did it look like?"

"You trying to be a smartass, son? What do you think a wolf looks like? Use your imagination. I saw him jump on a bike and take off through the woods before I passed out."

"Was the bike orange?"

"Yeah," Eli said with an excited nod. "So you know which wolf I'm talkin' about!"

"In fact, I do. He's bitten other people as well. I'm actually on the hunt for him. Any idea where he's headed?"

"Home. I told him about a shortcut through the backwoods behind my house."

Eli gave Gray the same directions. The detective outstretched his hand in a gesture of thanks. Eli shook it and smiled, exposing a handful of rotten teeth.

"I appreciate your help, Eli, but I have to get back on the road. I need to confiscate the van and agent Spac — err, the wolf's possessions. I will alert the authorities of what transpired here and your bravery."

"No problem, sonny. Just leave the bodies with me. I'll make sure they get a proper burial. Can't be leaving dead wolves out to rot in the sun. You never know when they're going to go all zombie on ya."

"Uh, thanks, Eli. And remember to take care of that wound."

"What are you, my mother? Fuck off and get off my land."

"Yes, sir."

Gray searched the body of his temporary partner, giving it a quick pat down and turning out his pockets. He pocketed Spacek's badge, wallet, keys and a worn book of matches. After picking his service pistol up off the ground, Gray took a deep breath, grabbed Jeremiah's body by the ankles and dragged him out of the van. The heavy-set man's body made a large thump sound when it hit the ground. Gray didn't like the idea of leaving the bodies with a madman, but he didn't want to provoke a firefight with the person that just saved his life. He also knew he had no jurisdiction over this crime, and would get tied up for countless hours with local authorities over what just transpired. Gray also wanted to avoid the locals due to Spacek's relationship with Sergeant Paperneau. Is Paperneau working with Spacek? Did he know Spacek's plans for me? A dozen different what-ifs played out in Gray's mind as he hopped behind the wheel of the van and turned the keys. It was 12:05 a.m.

Gray drove for ten minutes using Eli's directions then stopped the van and turned on his hazard lights. He tried to use Spacek's cell phone to call Crump but couldn't get past the six-digit pass code, rendering it useless. He threw the phone to the passenger-side floor in frustration, and then continued to search the vehicle. Gray was unsurprised that he was unable to find his phone. He figured it was the first thing Spacek would have ditched back at the C.O.S.T.C.O. to avoid any possible tracking by the TPD. Gray found Spacek's silenced pistol, along with his backup Betty and a few old napkins under the driver's seat. He strapped Betty on to his ankle, picked up Spacek's pistol with a napkin and placed it in the glove box. He opened Spacek's wallet and thumbed through its contents. Gray found forty-five dollars in the billfold, a driver's license, a credit card bearing the name Edward Spacek, and a folded up piece of paper in one of the pockets. Upon unfolding the document, the detective's eyes lit up and his heart pounded. It was a notice of termination of services from utility giant Toronto HyPrice due to unpaid electricity bills, and it didn't belong to Spacek. Gray smiled as he stared at the delinquent account addressed to an apartment in Mississauga's east end.

"Hello, Remy Delemme," Gray said to himself as he put the van back into drive, slammed his foot down on the gas pedal and headed back towards Toronto.

12

HOOTS AND TAILS

With the wind in my hair and bug splatter on my cheeks, I drove down Highway 7 towards my final destination. Every time I passed a road sign showing the distance to Toronto I grew increasingly excited, like a child counting down the days until Christmas morning. Finishing my quest and seeing Rose again were my only concerns. Now that I had the tools to complete my mission I felt like a lion stalking its prey. I always loved lions, especially the males. They live to fight, eat and mate with as many female lions as possible. One could argue those fearsome felines and I are one and the same. Well, we would be if I could get anyone to mate with me, and I suppose I don't really showcase dominance over anyone. Hmm. Perhaps I'm more like a panda. Those docile creatures never get laid and I don't think they showcase any dominance in the animal kingdom. Yes, I am a panda. A fat and lazy panda. I'm so cute and fluffy. As I discovered my inner animal, I drove past the well-lit welcome sign for Toronto. I had no idea how late it was, nor did I care. I almost peed myself from the combination of excitement and five hours of driving without a bathroom break.

"Yeah, baby!" I yelled as I passed the sign, swallowing a bug. The foul taste of the bug made me gag, so I pulled off the highway and parked my bike at a 24-hour Tim Hooter's. Back when I was a young lad, my father would take me to these fine, upscale eateries. I remember him telling me about how this franchise was once two separate businesses. He told me that the restaurants had merged to combat the rising success of high-end coffee houses and greasy gentlemen-only social clubs. Oh Dad, you always made up such silly stories. I mean seriously, how could no one ever think of selling coffee and tender, luscious breasts together until 2026? My train of thought was derailed as I entered the restaurant and walked up to the ordering station. I was greeted by a beautiful, busty blonde woman in a low-cut tank top.

"Welcome to Tim Hooter's, how may I service you?"

I took me a few seconds to look her in the eyes to place my order.

"Hey there, beautiful. I'd like one Combo No. 3 with an extra-large squirrelly fries and a large coffee."

As I waited for the cost of my meal to be rung up I could smell the scent of a fresh pot of coffee combined with the delectable aroma of a fresh No.3 hot off the grill.

"That will be $22.95, handsome," the woman said with a well-rehearsed smile.

Although I am normally against paying $22.95 for a single meal, I felt it was time to treat myself. After all, it's not like I would be requiring money in the near future. Besides, nothing tastes better than a couple of cutesy woodland creatures in the middle of the night. I snagged my combo from the voluptuous vixen at the cash and shoved a handful of deep-fried squirrel tails into my mouth. I followed the tails up with a big bite from one of my two burgers, making my taste buds rejoice. I love owl burgers!

After devouring my meal I remembered my inklin' for a tinklin' and ran to the bathroom. As I made my way inside I realized my need for a number one was now joined by its friend, number two. And unlike number one, number two was an impatient bastard. I clenched my buttocks and lunged into a stall while unzipping my jeans. My pants fell down to my ankles as I flopped onto the greasy restaurant toilet seat. I gripped the toilet paper dispenser with my left hand while my right attempted to hold on to the stall wall, as my pocket rockets left orbit in a hurry. After a few uncomfortable minutes, I let out a relieving sigh as my hands and stomach began to relax. I slid my hand around the left wall in an effort to locate the toilet paper. My hand came into contact with an empty plastic spindle. I looked behind me to check the top of the bowl for a loose roll and found nothing. Fucksticks.

In a desperate search for a few errant sheets, I realized I was not alone. I could see part of a shoe sticking out of the stall to my right.

"Hey buddy, could you help a brother out and toss me a roll?" I asked, hoping the guy wouldn't be a jerk and ignore my plea.

"How about I give you a hot dog instead you stupid prick!" the man yelled back in a familiar voice.

No, it couldn't be. As I attempted to calculate the odds of the man next to me being someone I met on my quest, my ears were flooded with the sounds of a cackling old man running out of the restroom, presumably with all the toilet paper. Double fucksticks. I lunged out of the stall after the old man, but tripped on my pants which were still hanging around my ankles, and fell face first into a garbage can. After removing a few soiled tissues from my scalp, I grabbed hold of the closest counter and pulled myself to my feet. Choosing between used tissues and no paper I decided to opt for the paperless option. I sat my soiled behind in the sink and turned on the taps. As

I splashed lukewarm water on my behind, a middle-aged man and his young boy opened the door to the bathroom.

"Daddy, why is that man washing his bum in the sink?" the child asked as his father's eyes lit up with rage, obviously upset that his son was subjected to this grotesque scene.

"There's been a T.P. robbery. Someone call the manager before this place goes poopsageddon," I said, defending my actions.

The middle-aged man ushered his boy out of the bathroom and called for a manager.

"Where's the manager? Some guy is shitting in the sink!" the boy's father yelled.

"Lies!" I yelled back through the door. "I'm just washing my ass!"

I hopped off the sink and tried to dry my buttocks using the jet engine-powered hand dryer. The heat from the hand dryer singed the hair on my buttocks and I yelped in pain as a manager burst through the door. He ran out as quickly as he came inside.

"Jesus, now he's having some sort of kinky sex with the hand dryer," he yelled. "Call the police!"

Jesus. Can't a man clean himself without getting the cops involved?

There was a small window open above one of the stalls in the bathroom leading to the parking lot, so I decided to hop on the toilet and pull myself through. My wiry frame barely fit through the window. The back of my shoe kicked the window on my way out, shattering the glass, as I fell into a dumpster below. The smell of old owl meat and squirrel tails filled my nostrils as I waded through the trash and made my way out of the waste bin. I ran to my bike, hopped on, and started the engine as the manager spotted me. He ran outside and shouted obscenities as I peeled out of the lot and got back on the road. That's the last time I go out of my way to grab a pair of hooters and a little tail while I'm on the road. It's not worth the trouble. I passed an electronic billboard on the road that showed the time to be 3:40 a.m. Perfect. I could still make the discothèque.

* * * *

Gray weaved through winding dirt roads until he hit Autoroute 50, which he took to the NQ-148 West, crossing over the Ottawa River and onto Highway 17 just outside of Arnprior. After barrelling down Highway 29 to Highway 7, he drove on to Highway 15 and stopped at a 24-hour service station in Smiths Falls. Gray filled the van, bought a prepaid cell phone, and tore out of the gas station as fast as the vehicle could muster, while dialing his partner's number. Crump's cell rang until it sent Gray to his voicemail. Gray called it again, hoping it would wake his slumbering partner. It was 3:35 a.m.

"Hello," said a half-asleep John Crump. His voice was partially muffled due to half his face being sunk into a pillow.

"Crump, it's Gray. Wake the hell up," his mentor replied. Crump immediately sat up, pulling the bed sheet off Monica, exposing the lower half of her buttocks that stuck out of the detective's t-shirt, which she was now wearing. Crump took a moment to admire her backside before placing the bed sheet back over her.

"Crump!" Gray yelled into the phone, cursing the thought of his partner being half in the bag or in the middle of a sexual encounter with some tramp he picked up at his local watering hole.

"I'm here, boss," Crump replied while hopping out of bed and looking around in a mad scramble for his pants. "What's going on? Where the hell have you been all this time?"

Crump's questions didn't even begin to stir Monica, who was out like a light from the combination of painkillers and an enthusiastic performance from the young detective that left her comfortably numb, wrapped up in an oversized death metal t-shirt.

Gray spent ten minutes updating Crump on everything that had transpired over the past couple of days: the C.O.S.T.C.O., Spacek's betrayal and the identification of the suspect. At this point, Crump had slipped out of the reporter's apartment and was running down the hall to the stairs in blue jeans, a gun holster and no shirt.

"Holy shit, that cocksucker tried to kill you?" Crump said completely shocked by the wave of news that Gray just hit him with.

"Yeah, and he spoke as if there was an entire organization out looking for our suspect, and that they weren't interested in arresting him."

"What the hell would they want him for if they're not going to arrest him?"

"Good question, rookie. We need to find Delemme before they do. Spacek's crew probably has the apartment under surveillance already, and our perp could show up any minute."

"What should I do if Spacek's boss is still hanging out in Gleeb's office? What if he is part of this?"

"This doesn't sound like any sort of F.B.I. investigation Crump, but just in case, go to Gleeb's house and wake him up. Tell him everything I just told you."

"You got it, boss. Where are you?"

"I'm still a few hours outside the city limits. Don't wait for me. Just find Gleeb and convince him to assemble a team to hit the apartment. I'll meet you there as soon as I can."

"Sure thing, boss."

"By the way, how's the I.D. going on Monica's attacker?"

"So far we haven't found any suspects that match. Could be unrelated. Her face is pretty recognizable and reporters sometimes have their share of enemies."

"True. Keep me posted if you hear anything. How's she doing?"

Crump smiled and blushed when Gray asked about Monica. If Gray was standing in front of him, he would have known about Crump's sexcapades instantly. Instead, he had to wait three seconds.

"I've been with her since I got into the city. She's feeling a lot better, boss, especially since her last dose of penis-cillin."

"Jesus, Crump, are you fucking her again? She's a victim in a crime, for God's sake."

"I know, boss. I'll be careful."

"What you'll be is celibate until I get back. Fuck another victim and I'll neuter you myself. Now go wake Gleeb and call me back," Gray said angrily as he hung up the phone.

"Yes, sir," Crump responded, knowing full well his mentor was no longer on the other line.

When Gray was angry and ranting he had a tendency to be over dramatic, but that didn't stop Crump from worrying about his little man. He knew he crossed the line by sleeping with Monica, but everyone has a weakness, and Crump's was women of the Monica variety. Nothing got Crump hotter than a smart, sexy and sassy woman.

Crump grabbed his doughnut jelly-stained t-shirt from Spacek's SUV, which he had slacked on returning to the precinct. He hopped behind the wheel and began driving towards his captain's home. Crump decided to try calling his captain while he was on the road. Gleeb answered before the second ring finished.

"Captain Gleeb speaking."

"Captain, it's John Crump. I need—"

"It's almost 4 a.m.," his superior replied, interrupting the detective. "You better have a good reason for waking me up at this time of night. Did you I.D. Burke's attacker?"

"No, sir, I have urgent news from Detective Gray. We need to meet up immediately — alone."

"What the hell are you talking about, Crump? You know this is a joint investigation. I have to keep the F.B.I. informed of all on-goings with the case."

"They may be part of the problem, sir. Agent Spacek wasn't what he pretended to be."

Gleeb realized Crump's sense of urgency when he used past tense to discuss the F.B.I. agent.

"Meet me at the precinct in fifteen minutes, detective. I want a full debriefing."

"There's no time, sir. We have to mo—"

"Don't try and give me orders, rookie. We do things by the book at Division 22. Just get your ass over there, pronto."

"You're the boss, Captain."

Crump cursed out his boss after he carefully checked to make sure the call had been disconnected. The young detective jumped on the highway and headed over to Division 22, hoping that Gray was putting the pedal to the metal. Crump knew the clock was ticking.

13

Man's Greatest answer

As I drove past the pair of mustard yellow buildings I called home, I could feel my quest coming quickly to its end. I could picture Rose dancing around the kitchen in her pink boy shorts, pulling an all-nighter with a bottle of tequila and a good first-person shooter on her Y-Box videogame console. We spent countless nights blowing each other up and filling each other with lead over pizza and booze. Nights well wasted, I thought.

Soon, Rose. I'll be home soon. Keep my controller warm for me, I thought to myself as I parked my bike a few buildings down from our home at the Dirty Beaver Disco.

The brickwork holding up the nightclub was old and crumbling. It was covered in scorch marks from the grease fires that had broken out at the club over its lifetime. The club averaged a new owner every twelve to twenty-four months, most likely due to its clientele. The nightclub was open until 5 a.m. and generally entertained the greasiest of customers — people looking for a last-minute lay, paid or unpaid, or a quick score. Although the club was well known to local police due to the brawls, shootings and drug deals that took place there, it wasn't all bad. It had fifty-cent chicken drumsticks every Tuesday at noon. Rose and I liked to frequent the establishment once a week for lunch.

Even at 4:15 a.m. on a Sunday, the nightclub had a long lineup to get inside. A large, muscular man with bronzed skin and slicked back hair stood guard at the entrance with his arms crossed. He was wearing a serious don't-fuck-with-me look. He sported the standard bouncer's uniform of a tight black t-shirt, dress pants and a solid gold chain around his neck.

Before heading inside the discotheque I opened up my bag to review my inventory: one box of waterproof matches, one pair of night vision goggles, one fake wax moustache, and greasy blue coveralls, compliments of Jeremiah. I rolled my eyes upon the discovery of a change of clothes. If I knew I had something like this lying around I wouldn't have gone to all that trouble to wash my ass. I ducked between cars in the parking lot and changed into the coveralls. They had Jeremiah's name sewn into one of the chest pockets. Now I'm ready, I thought.

I snuck around the side of the building into an alley. There were about six small windows on the side of the building. I peered into each one until I came upon the window for the women's bathroom. I peeked in and saw old, broken marble floors, graffiti-covered stall doors and rusty taps attached to filthy sinks. The bathroom was a wreck, so I didn't think anyone would mind if I added to the décor. I picked up a brick and tossed it through the window, then made my getaway through the opposite end of the alley where the discotheque's loading dock was located. The dock smelled of old vomit and rotten beer. A seemingly endless number of old wooden barrels littered the area. A red, five-ton truck with the words Beer Bus painted in yellow on its sides was idling at the back entrance. There were no workers in sight. They were probably checking out the noises that came from the women's bathroom. This was the perfect opportunity to sneak inside the building. I dragged one of the wooden barrels half-filled with old rainwater over to the side door of the delivery truck, removed the lid, hopped inside the container and placed the lid firmly on top. The bass being generated from the music inside the club vibrated the barrel. I was so focused on the vibrations I didn't hear the dock worker's footsteps as he approached me.

"Hey Joey, how many times do I gotta tell you to stop leavin' fuckin' barrels lying around?" the worker yelled.

"Fuck off, Frankie! I'm on lunch!" Joey replied.

"Fuckin' lazy mook," Frankie mumbled to himself as he picked up my barrel and hoisted it onto his shoulder.

"Phew, this barrel fuckin' stinks," Frankie said as he carried me inside the club.

I held my breath and closed my eyes as the stale water splashed my face. Less than a minute later, Frankie placed the barrel on the ground. Thankfully, I was right side up.

"Joey, you best be done eatin' if you know what's good for ya," I heard Frankie yell.

"Frankie, why don't you eat me, huh?" Joey yelled. "Someone just broke the women's bathroom window. Why don't you be a good little bitch and call somebody to clean this shit up?"

"That's it you little punk — it's time to teach you some respect!" Franke replied as the sounds of his footsteps went out of earshot.

I popped the lid off the barrel and stuck my head out to get acquainted with my new surroundings. I had been placed in a walk-in beer cooler. I was surrounded by wooden barrels of alcohol and cases of beer. Frankie had left the door to the cooler wide open, presumably to make stocking the rest of the delivery easier on him. I could hear Joey and Frankie's heated exchange in the distance. They sounded like they were going to come to blows. I grabbed two cans of beer and stuffed them into my coveralls before exiting the cooler, figuring I would need a drink or two to help me with the hard work still to come.

The two men were now screaming at each other in Italian. I took this opportunity to swipe a janitor's cleaning cart that was sitting in the hallway. I felt like I was in a film, infiltrating the enemy's base to find out vital information that would help save the day. The theme song from an old secret agent movie began to echo in my head as I attached my fake moustache. The moustache covered my nostrils and upper lip, brushing the middle of my cheeks. It was a mighty moustache!

As I pushed the cleaning cart down the hall I could see the outlines of two giant, ape-like men in the distance. They both sported uninviting frowns as I approached them. It was time to get into character. Thank the gods for the mighty 'stache. While approaching the two behemoths, I decided it would be best to attempt talking to them in their native accents.

"Aw, fungula!" I said making several angry motions with my hands. "Who-make-a-da-mess, huh? I jus' clean-a-da place and they dirty it up! Gimme a couple-a-minutes, okay."

The two men nodded in approval of my wild hand gestures and angry rant. I wheeled the cart past them and entered the ladies' bathroom. I closed the bathroom door and searched for a place to position myself for my mission. One of the ceiling panels above the sink was moved out of place, leaving the pipes exposed. It was perfect! I hopped onto the counter and grabbed a two-inch thick steel pipe, hoping it wouldn't burn my hands. The metal was cold to the touch. I pulled myself into the ceiling and slid the panel back into place, leaving only a small opening for one of my eyes to see through. Now all I needed to do was wait.

After five minutes, the door burst open to reveal Frankie.

"Eh, Joey, where the hell is that mook wit' da mops?" he yelled to his co-worker.

"Fuck off, Frankie, I'm on a smoke break!" Joey replied.

"Dammit, Joey, you lazy bastard!" Frankie yelled while slamming the door.

The sound of the two men arguing was followed up with the smashing of furniture and more angry-sounding Italian. I'm going to miss these two when the bombs fall.

My body was sandwiched between pipes and ceiling tiles and I was surrounded by dead rodents. The scent was unpleasant. I attempted to shift my body so my mouth could take in a little fresh air from the hole in the ceiling tile, but I raised my head too fast and smashed the back of my skull on a large steel pipe. Everything became dark.

An unknown amount of time passed before I awoke to the sounds of drunken female laughter and ear-piercing country-disco. I took a deep breath, calmed my nerves, and listened intensely as I placed my eye through the peep hole. After all my efforts, I was finally going to uncover the truth, once and for all. I will finally be at peace.

There were five inebriated women standing in a circle. They were all dressed in different coloured short skirts and boots. One of the women had her back facing me and her arm stretching high into the air pointing at the ceiling. She had blonde hair and wore a pink skirt, black boots, a black tank top, and a spiked necklace.

"Alright now, who wants it?" she yelled while the other four women laughed and shouted, as they all attempted to grab the hand of the woman speaking.

"Give it to me, baby," one of the women shouted. "It's time to tear it up!"

"Alright then, this one is for you, bitch!" the woman in pink said as she brought her arm down and pointed at the other woman.

And with that, my question was answered. Of course! Why hadn't I ever figured it out before? The answer was so simple. So obvious. All my life I tortured myself trying to figure out why women go to bathrooms in groups, and now I finally knew!

The chosen woman grabbed on tightly to the other woman's finger and gave it a strong tug as the sound of panty poofs erupted. A "Pshhhhhhhhhh-ratta-tatta-tat" sound, followed by a small squeak filled the room, much to the joy of all the women.

"Nice one!" the finger-tugger said while laughing and giving the woman in pink a high five. The occupants of the bathroom erupted in celebration as the foul stench filled the room. Overcome with joy from fulfilling my quest, I pushed the ceiling tile out of the way and shouted in victory while pointing at the group of deceitful harpies.

"Aha, I knew it!"

Their heads all shot up as they gazed in horror at the infiltration of their once impenetrable lair. That's when I realized the danger I was in. The five women knew they just got the entire female race busted. Women think farts are funny, too, and now a man knew it. He would have to be dealt with.

"Frankie!" one of the women screamed. "There's a pervert with a huge moustache in the ceiling!"

Sensing a serious beating approaching my already bruised posterior, I pleaded with them to calm down.

"Wait, I wasn't trying t—"

Forgetting that my accent was still in angry hand gesture mode, I accidently knocked another ceiling tile loose, sending me plummeting towards the angry mob below. Fortunately, my fall was broken by the five hoochies, who now lay stunned under my carcass. Before they could gather their wits, I jumped to my feet and climbed through the window I had broken earlier, cutting my right hand in the process. My body came crashing down on the back of a homeless man who was slumbering peacefully in the alley. I ripped the moustache from my lips and placed it on his as compensation for waking him up before running like a scared little girl out of the alley. By the time I reached the end of the alley I was met by Joey and Frankie. I froze on the spot as they charged in my direction. Well, I guess this it. My time has finally come. I closed my eyes and awaited my fate.

"Eh, get outta da way you, mook," Frankie said, shoving me aside.

I opened my eyes to witness Frankie and Joey make their way towards the confused homeless man.

"So, you like to peep on women takin' shits, huh? You fuckin' perv," Joey yelled as he punched the homeless man in the face.

"I don't know what you're talking about," the man said as he cowered and turtled into a defensive position.

"You think we're fuckin' stupid? You think just anybody can have a fuckin' moustache like that?" Joey screamed as he kicked the man in his ribs.

I ran through the parking lot and hustled home on foot, abandoning my bike in the process. Thoughts of Rose filled my head as I ran home for one last chance to be together.

* * * *

By the time the clock on the van's radio hit 5:30 a.m., Gray had already driven down Highway 15 to the westbound 401 and was quickly approaching the Toronto area. He had the van moving at speeds not designed for the beaten-up vehicle when it was brand new. He prayed to himself that the van would hold together long enough for him to get into the city limits. There were very few cars to pass at that time of the morning. His biggest fear was hitting a deer at that speed, which could have easily killed him, but Gray took his chances. He knew how close he was to finding his suspect, and that a shadow player probably had the jump on him. Gray almost ran out of fuel as he approached Whitby. The van was guzzling gas at a record pace due to Gray's blatant disregard for posted speed limits. He called Crump for an update as he filled up at a highway service station.

"Boss?" Crump answered.

"What's going on, Crump? Fill me in, pronto."

"I'm at the precinct with Gleeb. He's assembling a full S.W.A.T. team to hit the apartment, but there's a problem."

Gray cursed to himself, suspecting he already knew the cause for the delay.

"Gleeb called the F.B.I., didn't he?" he said.

"You got it, boss. They're creating a clusterfuck of red tape. Our suspect could be long gone, or in the hands of Spacek's people by the time our unit gets deployed."

"Jesus. Alright, rookie, then you're on."

"Say what now?"

"Slip out the back while Gleeb is busy dealing with the F.B.I. and get over to the apartment and stake it out. Were you able to get a photo of the perp?"

"Yeah, but it wasn't easy."

"What do you mean? Didn't you scroll through the city's database?" Gray asked as he jumped back into the van and peeled out of the service station.

"Of course, boss, but his photo wasn't in any database. He doesn't have a driver's license, passport or any other type of Glamerican-issued photo I.D."

"So how did you I.D. him?"

"A couple of our boys over in Division 27 were emailing around a video for laughs of a guy suspected of shitting in a sink at a Tim Hooter's. When they mentioned that the guy took off on an orange bike I asked them to send any video they had. It's not the clearest, but he's definitely a white male, around six feet tall. He's got a mess of shaggy brown hair and he's wearing–"

"Blue jeans and a purple t-shirt," Gray said, interrupting Crump's description.

"You got it, boss. I haven't had a chance to share this with Gleeb yet."

"Is Special Agent Mincer with him now?"

"No. They've been yelling at each other over the phone for the better part of an hour. I don't know who this guy is, but Gleeb doesn't want to move without his say-so."

"Then fuck him. Gleeb just doesn't want to risk screwing up his early retirement. Get down to that apartment and keep me posted on anything suspicious. I'll be there soon."

"You got it, boss."

Gray continued to push the van to its limits as he raced down the highway towards the suspect's apartment, trying to put the pieces together. Gray had always been a pro at solving puzzles, but the apparent randomness of Delemme's crimes were making it difficult to profile him. And why was he in such a rush to get home? The deceased mechanic mentioned that Delemme was in a panic to get back home, and that he had done some sort of deal with a possible arms trafficker at the C.O.S.T.C.O. Did he intend to use whatever he purchased on someone in his apartment building? And what the hell was Spacek's play? The fallen agent murdered an innocent man and tried to kill a police detective to cover it up. Who was he working for? Gray narrowly avoided rear-ending a small sedan as he approached the Scarborough area. He decided to focus on the road for the rest of the trip until he met up with Crump at the apartment.

14

THE FINAL STEP

"I knew it! I knew it! I knew it!" I yelled as I ran back home to Rose. My body was shaking from the combination of anticipation to see her and adrenalin from my latest close encounter. I stopped at a bus shelter next to our apartment building and sat for a moment to catch my breath. Even my excitement to see Rose before the world came to an end couldn't muster me up enough lung power to counter eleven years of inhaling tobacco, tar and nicotine. Besides, the break would do me well. I needed a smoke. I lit one up and took a deep drag, then leaned back against the bus shelter's glass window and exhaled. With the exception of a slight pain in my chest, I felt better immediately. While puffing my life away, I reminisced about some of my happiest moments with Rose, including the one brief but intense moment of sexual passion we shared.

We had been living as roommates for about two years after my lease was revoked due to non-payment of rent. Rose and I were the best of friends. We spent many long nights drinking while doing battle in various video game arenas. During one particularly heavy night of drinking and joystick thumbing, I decided the time was right to share my feelings with Rose. I grabbed her by the back of her head, gripped onto a lock of her raven black hair, and pulled her close for a passionate kiss. Unfortunately, my hair pull was a little too passionate, as we ended up colliding heads and falling off the couch — although our lips did touch! Lying in a daze on our living room floor in a drunken stupor, I blurted out "I love you, Rose!" She pounced on top of me and in a slurred speech said, "Remy, I love you, too. Let's eat pizza," then kissed me. We tore at each other's clothes in a passionate, drunken affair that left me naked, satisfied and smiling forty-three seconds later. Rose, still lying on top of me, just as naked but less satisfied, explained that our love turned out to be plutonic and she was going to pursue people of the same gender for her sexual encounters for the rest of her life. I nodded my head and challenged her to a Y-Box hockey tournament over pizza. She planted a big, wet kiss on my lips then got dressed. We played hockey for the rest the night, and we remained just as close friends up until present day — maybe even closer. Besides, what does sex matter when you have a love this great?

After stomping out the remainder of my smoke with my shoe, I walked into our apartment building, hopped on the elevator, and smiled as I watched the dimly lit buttons make their way to the seventh floor. When the elevator reached our floor I could hear Rose's laughter echoing through the hallway, bouncing off the rusty orange paint that covered the walls. She was probably entertaining herself with old cartoons again. Few things made Rose happier on early mornings than sitting back and laughing at the antics of talking, shape-shifting robots and smack-talking soldiers. As I walked down the hall I stared at the stained retro-styled carpet that was stapled to the floor. There was something about that out-of-date, red spiral patterned carpet that forced my eyes to stare at it the whole walk to our apartment. When I got to the big round burn mark in the carpet — a brew-your-own-beer experiment gone horribly wrong — I knew I was home.

I unlocked the front door and walked inside. Rose was sitting in a folding chair meant for camping in our living room. She was wearing tight pink boy shorts, blue striped socks, and a light blue undershirt with no bra. Non-plutonic thoughts entered my mind about her for the millionth time as I ran to greet her. She was drinking a beer and playing Y-Box. She paused her game and looked up just in time for me to scoop her out of her chair and embrace her in a big bear hug. Rose squealed happily and wrapped her legs around my waist, giving my ribs a tight squeeze with her toned thighs. I groaned from the discomfort coming from my potentially cracked ribs, but only for a moment, as the sweet smell of Rose's black hair washed the pain away. She rested her forehead on mine and placed her lips less than an inch from my mouth. Like a horny sucker I took the bait and placed my lips on hers, only to have my lungs filled with a massive beer-fuelled belch. I coughed and tried to release her, but Rose's grip was tight. I stumbled over the folding chair and fell backwards to the floor, whacking the back of my head, while Rose's weight knocked the wind out of me. Dazed and gasping for breath, I pushed Rose off me. She laughed as she rolled off my bruised and battered torso. Rose held my hand and squeezed as she stared at me and smiled.

"Hi, Remy. Long time no see."

"Hey, Rose," I said, still trying to catch my breath. "It's good to see you."

"Where you been the last few days? And where's our couch? Not to mention all the rest of your stuff. Did you trade your furniture for chicken and ribs again?" she asked in a slightly disappointed tone, but still smiling.

"Nah, nothing that crazy. I was just completing a quest while preparing for the apocalypse."

"Oh, Remy," she replied with a sigh. "You're off your meds again, aren't you? I just hope you tried to stay out of trouble."

Rose is such a cutie. Always so paranoid over nothing. I guess she can't help it, she loves me. But it still strikes me as silly. Since when do I get into any real trouble? Rose gave my forehead a soft kiss, jumped to her feet and outstretched her arm towards me. I grabbed her hand and she pulled my torso up, so I was sitting on the floor.

"Alright, my little troublemaker," she said. "So what was your quest about this time?"

"Wouldn't you and the rest of the women on the planet like to know? I'm on to your games."

Rose stared at me with one eyebrow raised, displaying an impish grin.

"I guess you've caught all of us women red-handed," she said as she gave my head a noogie.

As Rose smiled at me I realized the absurdity of my quest. I laughed out loud hysterically, catching Rose off guard.

"Are you going to tell me what's so funny, crazy man?"

I shook my head and smiled.

"Nothing, Rose. Nothing at all."

After pulling myself to my feet, I walked onto our balcony and lit up the last smoke from the stale pack that was still sitting on my windowsill. As I stared out at the Mississauga skyline I realized what a fool I had been these past few days. What purpose was answering man's greatest question really going to serve with the end of days coming so soon? Being with Rose is all that ever mattered. I pulled the crumpled piece of paper containing my quest out of my pocket and opened it up.

My eyes scanned the tattered document until they met with the one item on the list I hadn't completed over my time on the road. *Number seven: find true love.*

"Done!" I said to myself as I gave my list a final stamp, crumpled up the piece of paper, stuffed it into the old cigarette pack and threw it off my balcony. I watched it get blown about in the wind on the way down until it eventually made contact with the pavement below. Only a few metres from where it landed, I could see a man leaning against a black SUV looking up at the apartments. He appeared to be holding a pair of binoculars, but it was hard to tell. "Friggin' pervert," I said to myself, catching

Rose's attention. She stuck her right arm out of our living room window and gave my bum a pinch.

"You rang, sir?" she said, while trying to sound like an old Englishman.

I smiled back, flicked my cigarette off the balcony and went inside. A second folding chair was awaiting my buttocks as I walked back inside our apartment. Rose was already back in her chair, drinking a beer and holding her joystick.

"Come play with me, Remy," she said in a seductive tone as she patted the seat of the second folding chair. I sat down and placed my arm around her. Rose placed her beer and joystick on the ground and nuzzled her head into my arm. She gazed up into my eyes for a moment before whispering softly into my ear, "You know, I have another game we could play, Remy."

I looked at her and smiled.

"It's been a long time, hasn't it?" I said.

"It has, Remy. Too long," she replied.

"I was planning on asking you before our time was up, but–"

"But nothing," Rose said, interrupting me. "You know I'm always up for a wild ride. Especially if the world is coming to an end," she said as she playfully bit my nipple.

"Even if we have to take that ride together?" I asked.

"Especially if we take that ride together," she replied.

"We are a good team, aren't we, Rose?"

"The best. Now buckle up, bitch."

And with that, we wrapped our bodies tightly around one another, hearts beating with anticipation, as our movements accelerated us towards what could very well be our final blaze of glory. This was the day we would make it down the seventh step, and we would make it together.

15

ONE REMY TO GO

I could feel a light breeze against my face as Rose and I barrelled towards our stairs of destiny.

"This is it, baby," I said. "The seventh step is ours for the taking."

Before Rose could respond we hit the first step and our combined weight collapsed the base of the rolly-chair, hurdling our bodies down the remainder of the staircase. Rose gripped herself tightly around my body to cushion herself from most of the blows, using my torso and groin as a barrier between her and the unforgiving steps. I closed my eyes and screamed like a five-year-old girl the entire way down the staircase. After our trip came to a bone-crunching halt, Rose placed her forefingers and thumbs on my eyelids and opened them up.

"Let's get pizza!" she said in an excited tone.

It took a few moments for me to muster a response, and even then, it was only a collection of semi-conscious groans. After a few minutes, Rose placed her lips close to my ear and gently slid her tongue across my ear lobe, making my body tingle. The pervy gesture shook enough of the cobwebs loose from my brain to ensure I was aware enough to absorb the thundering sound of Rose's belch-talk.

"Pizzaaaaaa!" she belched into my ear.

My reply of "Ungh-ll-make-call" was well received.

"Sweet," she said. "Just remember, your half gets no onions. Last time I nearly vomited in my sleep. Now stop napping, Remy, so we can get some pre-pizza drinking in. I've got a hankerin' for some flank-er-in," which was Rose's way of saying she wanted to play alien war games on Y-Box.

How could I argue with such a perfect combination of brains, beauty and belches? It was no surprise that I had been putty in her hands from the start. There was no better way for me to spend the rest of my life.

"Sure thing, Rose. Help me up so we can get drunk and I can wake up naked feeling dirty."

Rose giggled as she helped me up. We walked back up the flight of stairs and went back inside our apartment. Rose made the call to Pookie's Pizzeria as I grabbed us each a beer from the fridge. I made sure to give Rose's beer a firm shake before bringing it to her. As we plopped back into our folding chairs, I handed Rose her beer, popped the cap off my bottle and motioned for a cheers. As Rose opened her bottle, beer shot out of the top, soaking her torso.

"Dammit, Remy!" she said as she jumped to her feet, dripping wet.

I was initially going to laugh, but the liquid had soaked right through her undershirt, exposing her like a college girl in a wet t-shirt contest. The miraculous view left me stunned. The only response I could muster was a slack-jawed smile. Rose rolled her eyes, and then slapped me upside my head. She peeled off her wet top, bent over, grabbed me by my hair, and rubbed my face into her wet chest. After two of the greatest seconds of my life she pushed me away, forcing me to fall off my chair.

"You wish you could have these babies," she said while cupping her own breasts.

"I will have all your babies," I responded, obviously not thinking straight.

"Oh shut it, you big perv, and keep a lookout for the pizza guy. Remember Remy, don't let the pizza guy in until the clock reads 5:55 a.m. so we can get it free. I'm going to hop in the shower."

As Rose made her way into the shower and turned the taps towards hot-and-moist naked chick, I defended my ability to waste people's time.

"Not a problem, Rose, you know I'm the stall master. Why if I was in the army, I'd be General Stallin'. If I were in porn, I'd be Remy DeLay. If I was a car, I'd be—"

BANG! BANG! BANG!

I looked at the clock and saw it was 5:53 a.m. Damn! The pizza man was early, and he had an iron fist.

"Remy Delemme," the voice on the other side of the door bellowed. "This is the F.B.I. We have a warrant for your arrest!"

BANG! BANG! BANG!

I scoffed at the pizza man's attempt to get me to open the door. This guy was pretty sly, but I had been playing the pizza delivery game for a long time.

"I would be more than happy to open the door for you, officer," I said, barely containing my laughter. "But would you mind passing some identification through the bottom of the door first? You never know what kind of weirdo you might encounter lurking outside your apartment at this time of the morning."

I could hear the faint sound of people mumbling. The pizza man wasn't alone. He had brought back up.

"Remy Delemme, this is your last chance. Open the door, now!"

My stomach began to ache from the laughter I was containing. I placed my hand over my mouth to hold in the giggles, but I started snorting uncontrollably. I checked the clock again. With less than a minute to go, I figured the pizza was as good as mine.

"No problem, officer. I'll open the door in forty seconds. No wait, thirty-nine, thirty-eight, thirty–"

"Hit it, Billy!"

Hit it, Billy?

Before I could decode the meaning, my door was kicked down. It fell on top of me, pinning me to the floor. A half-dozen large pizza men in black uniforms armed with automatic weapons entered the apartment and surrounded me. Terror filled my heart as the barrels of the deliverymen's weapons pressed against my face. Jesus, the pizza guys have gone postal!

One of the giant men in black placed their size thirteen boot on the door, close to my chin, then flashed a piece of paper at me.

"Remy Delemme, you're under arrest," he said.

I couldn't believe how competitive the pizza marketplace had become. I'd been threatened with the odd fist fight or special sauce with my next order, but never an armed assault team. I guess they were brought in to handle the worst of offenders, and I definitely could have qualified for that list. I've probably stalled my way to more than a dozen pizzas in the past month alone, let alone my lifetime record of free pizza deliveries. The companies must have created some sort of database to track down the offenders. Some sort of joint-pizza initiative. I tried to negotiate my way out of the predicament.

"Look, guys, I can pay for the pizza. What are the charges?"

The man standing on top of me produced a second document.

"How about multiple counts of first-degree murder, one count of first-degree heifercide, grand theft auto, trespassing and destruction of property? And that's just the start, tough guy."

The man was obviously holding the wrong piece of paper. Instead of drawing attention to his error, I stared blankly at him for a moment while I tallied up the damages.

"How's $24.50 sound?"

The delivery man glared at me in disgust before kicking the door off of me, and flipping me on my back.

"Look, guys," I said in an extremely respectful tone, realizing they were slapping handcuffs on me. "There is $18.50 in my pocket. It's yours for the taking. I'll have to owe you the other six bucks, but don't worry, I'm good for it."

My offer didn't impress them, so I made it more appealing.

"Alright, fine. Let's round what I owe you guys up to a full twenty-five dollars. Now how does that tickle your fancy?"

As the apparent leader of the group pulled me to my feet, one of the other men scratched their head at my offer.

"Wow, does that even count as a bribe, Sarge?"

"Doesn't matter, Gonzales. This scumbag is never going to see the light of day again."

As the men dragged me from my apartment, I leered at the one known as Gonzales to show my displeasure with his lack of customer service skills. He responded to my body language immediately.

"You want to say something to me, shit-rat?" he said, while cracking the knuckles in his right hand.

"Yes I do," I replied. "You just lost your tip!"

As the men dragged me down the hallway, we passed a delivery woman holding a pizza and wearing a Pookie's Pizzeria shirt and hat, a plaid green kilt and purple riding boots. Her face was covered by her cap as she walked by us, but long, red curly hair flowed from the hat down to the middle of her back. I turned my neck to the best of my abilities to check out her backside as she made her way towards my apartment door. While being dragged down the stairs, I could see our door open in the distance and the pizza woman step inside.

The enraged pizza men dragged me down the steps and out the front entrance, where they were confronted by three men flashing badges. Both groups immediately began to argue. The three men appeared to be blocking the path of the disgruntled delivery men. One of the men definitely looked like a cop. He was the oldest of the three, dressed in a blue blazer, white dress shirt and black tie. He appeared to be a figure of authority. The other two men were dressed in blue jeans and t-shirts. One of them wore a shirt covered in dried jelly stains.

* * * *

"Out of the way, boys, you missed the party," Sarge said to the three men.

"Blow me, roid rage," Crump replied. "That's our collar."

"I wouldn't talk collars if I were you," said Gonzales, referring to Crump's stained shirt. Gonzales then pulled a dollar coin from his pocket and tossed it to the rookie detective. "Here's a dollar, kid. Go buy yourself a new shirt."

"Why spend it on a shirt when I can buy your mother twice for the same price?" Crump replied, sparking a shoving match between himself and Gonzales.

"Calm down, detective," Gleeb said while restraining Crump.

A couple of the men in black lowered their weapons to restrain Gonzales. Gray took advantage of the chaos to get close to the suspect.

"Remy," he said, getting the suspect's attention, "you're not what they say you are, are you? What's really going on here? What's your play?"

"I just wanted a free pizza," Remy replied. "The world is coming to an end. I don't understand what the big deal is."

"Get away from him!" Sarge yelled as he drove his palm into the detective's face to shove him out of the way.

Gray surprised the larger man, batting his arm away with his right hand, then connecting with a left cross that caught Sarge flush on the chin. The larger man's knees buckled and he stumbled backwards, landing on his ass. A couple of Sarge's men raised their weapons at Gray in response. Crump pulled his service pistol and aimed it at Gonzales' Neanderthal-like head. Gleeb got between the two parties, arms outstretched, in an effort to avoid a shootout.

Remy stood there with one of the men in black and watched the chaos unfold.

"This is just like the movies," Remy said. "Do you have any candy or popcorn?"

"Shut it, moron, or I'll shut it for you," the man replied.

"Everybody calm the fuck down, now!" Gleeb yelled, catching everyone off guard. "Crump, lower your weapon — that's an order!"

After a few moments of tense silence, Crump lowered his weapon. The men in black did the same. Sarge got back to his feet and rubbed his chin.

"Nice punch you have there, detective," Sarge said. "Try that again and I'll kill you."

"My apologies, officer," Gray said. "That crossed a line. But that's our perp you have there, and he's coming with us."

"You have jelly doughnut on your shirt," Remy said while staring at Crump, interrupting Sarge.

"I said shut it," the man guarding Remy replied, slapping him upside his head.

"I like doughnuts," Crump replied. "You want to come down to the station with us and split a dozen? My treat."

"Doughnuts are good," Remy replied.

"He's not going anywhere, detective," Sarge said, pulling out a piece of paper and handing it to Gleeb. "I have orders from high up to bring him in, and they're signed off by your people and mine. This prick is headed to the promised land."

"Doughnut Land?" Remy asked.

"Prince Albert, jerk-off," Sarge replied.

"What's a Prince Albert?" Remy asked.

"You don't want to know," Gray replied.

Gleeb quickly scanned the document for signatures to see who was going to catch hell for this.

"Son of a bitch," Gleeb said, passing the document to Gray.

"What?" Crump asked. "Are we seriously going to let these clowns take our perp?"

Gray tried to control his rage as he crumpled the paper up.

"Let them pass, Crump," Gray said, moving out of their way.

"Are you serious, boss?" Crump asked, shocked that his mentor would give up after all their efforts to capture Delemme.

"It's signed by D.A. Helmer," Gray replied. "We no longer have jurisdiction."

"What? Seriously?" Crump said, flabbergasted.

"Yeah, let them through," Gray said, repeating his order. "We'll take this up with Helmer."

Gonzales grinned at Crump as he passed him, bumping shoulders with the rookie. Crump desperately wanted to shoot Gonzales in the ass with his pistol, but restrained himself. The men in black walked by the detectives and tossed Remy into the back of a blue van and drove away.

"What the hell just happened, Gray?" Crump asked, scratching his scalp.

"I don't know, kid, but we're going to find out."

* * * *

After tossing me into the van like a sack of potatoes, my handcuffs were removed momentarily so the armed men could shackle me to the floor of the van. Sarge and another one of the postal pizza men jumped into the front seats and started the engine, while the remaining men sat on steel benches lining the sides of the vehicle. The van was sparkling clean.

"Hey guys, this van is in immaculate condition. Who cleans this thing?" I asked.

"Keep it up, jerk-off, and I'll shut that mouth of yours permanently," Gonzales said.

"So where are we going?" I asked.

"HQ, jerk-off," Gonzales explained. "You've got a meeting with the big man."

"Which man?"

"What are you, retarded or something?" Gonzales asked. "I said you're meeting with the big man. The big cheese? The big kahuna? Any of these make sense to you?"

"I think so," I replied. "So I'm meeting with someone that's really fat?"

Gonzales raised the butt of his gun to hit me, but stopped when I stuck my arms out, gesturing for him to wait a moment while I changed my answer.

"Wait, wait. I totally get it now," I said. "You're talking about God! Wow! God runs Pookie's Pizzeria. This whole religion thing is really working out for him."

"Enough!" Gonzales screamed shortly before he rammed the butt end of his gun between my eyes. Everything went dark again.

* * * *

Gleeb, Gray and Crump all fired questions at each other while huddled around Spacek's black SUV in an attempt to make heads or tails of the scenario that just transpired in the parking lot. Gleeb scratched the top of his combover while staring at the document he had been presented minutes earlier.

"The F.B.I. rarely goes to this kind of trouble to pressure the local D.A. like this — especially when it's just to nab one perp," he said.

"How do you know Helmer was pressured?" Crump asked as he took a beat-up cigarette pack out of his jacket.

"Helmer doesn't give up high-profile cases, kid," Gleeb responded. "Trust me on that one. That Special Agent Jacob Mincer must be pretty special to the F.B.I. He really had a bug up his ass on this one."

"Something doesn't add up here. We're missing something," Gray said.

"Don't let it eat you up too bad, detective," Gleeb said. "In the end, we got a killer off the streets. That's one more serial killer locked away thanks to you."

"A killer, yes. But I don't think he's a serial. I think he's something else," Gray said.

"And what was Spacek's game? He had a partner in all of this," Gray said.

"Yeah, well, I'll get to the bottom of that, that's for damn sure!" Gleeb said, fired up at the thought of someone trying to take out one of his own. "I'm sure ol' scar face will find a way to cover his ass for teaming some psycho up with the TPD. He'll probably say the guy was depressed or some other bullshit. There's always some sort of bullshit when dealing with th–"

"Fuck me!" Crump said, as he dug through his pockets in a frenzy. He pulled out his cell phone so quickly it almost flew out of his hands.

"What is it, rookie?" Gray asked as he started to get an uneasy feeling in the pit of his stomach. It only reared its ugly head when he felt he missed something vital in a case, or when he let Crump choose their lunch spot.

"Monica's attacker," Crump replied. "The artist's rendering. They emailed it to me an hour ago. Monica said the attacker was the same guy she snapped photos of at our two murder scenes. Some guy with Washington plates. In all the chaos I forgot to forward it to you guys."

"Was it Spacek trying to cover his tracks?" Gleeb asked.

"No. I showed a photo of him to Monica and she said it definitely wasn't him," Crump replied as he thumbed through his email on his cell phone for a few seconds then held the screen up to Gray's face.

"This is the perp," he said.

Gray took the phone from his partner and held it up to Gleeb's face. The police Captain's skin turned pale, and his face looked grim.

"You know who this man is, don't you Captain?" Gray asked.

"Jesus," Gleeb responded.

"I highly doubt that," Crump said, waiting for his superior to finish his answer.

"Good God, that's Agent Mincer."

* * * *

When I awoke I was shackled to a chair in the middle of a small steel-walled room, approximately ten feet by ten feet. My chair and chains were the only objects in the room I could see. Someone had taken great care to give this room a no-streak shine. I should ask them to clean my windows.

A few minutes later, a door behind me opened and revealed a man dressed in a baby blue suit, white dress shirt and gold tie, holding a manila folder. He looked to be in his late thirties or early forties. He had dark, slicked-back hair and a chiseled face with a strong, square jawline and a large scar that ran from the bottom of his lip down his chin. He must have had an unfortunate accident with a pizza cutter at some point in his career with the company. The man grabbed a steel chair from behind my back and carried it over to the middle of the room, placing it in front of me. He sat down on the chair, pulled a pack of Cats from his suit jacket and lit one up, exhaling in my face.

"Hello, Remy," the man said, revealing a scratchy voice. "It's a pleasure to meet you. I've been eager to make your acquaintance. My name is Jacob Mincer."

"Hi Jacob, I like your tie."

Jacob smiled, unshackled one of my hands and offered me a cigarette. I happily took one. The scarred man gave me a light, then leaned back and opened his manila folder.

"I like you, Remy. I like what you can do. I can tell we're going to be good friends."

Jacob appeared to be a top dog in this organization. Only a man in a seat of great power could strut through the halls in a suit like his. He must be an assistant manager.

"I hope my cigarette brand is still to your liking, Remy," Jacob said as he browsed his folder.

"Totally, Jacob. They're actually my favourite brand."

"I had a feeling they were, Remy."

"How come?"

"Because you left a trail of them, like bread crumbs, over the last few days. We found them scattered all the way from here to the New Quebec border. Did you know the New Quebecers are currently battling an extremely destructive forest fire?"

"Yeah, I drove around it."

"If they can't get it under control, they stand to lose millions in syrup production. It's terrible how something as small as an errant cigarette butt can spark a forest fire of that magnitude during the dry season."

"I agree, Jacob. People need to be more careful."

Jacob grinned at my answer, finding something about it entertaining. I'm not sure what though. Forest fires are no laughing matter.

"This may come as a surprise to you, Remy, but the New Quebec government suspects you of starting that fire."

"Why would they think that?"

"Because I told them you did."

"Oh. Well that's weird, since I don't remember starting any fires."

"Weird indeed, Remy."

"So how mad are they? Are they going to fine me? Seems unfair since I'm pretty sure I didn't do it. But if it will bring peace between the two countries I suppose I can pay my fair share. I'll pay them twenty four dollars and fifty cents, but I'll need you to spot me six bucks."

"The New Quebec government is actually more interested in having us transfer you to them in a prisoner exchange. That way the New Quebecers could brand you a terrorist and have you executed."

"Hmm, sounds like a serious mix-up."

"Indeed. Of course, I told them we would handle the situation ourselves and that killing you would be unnecessary. At least, I hope it will be."

I nodded my head. What was this guy talking about?

"I think there's a case of mistaken identity happening here, chief. I was brought in for multiple freebie pizza offences. By the way, what does Pookie's Pizzeria have to do with the government?"

Jacob closed the manila folder and lit another cigarette for himself, this time without offering me one. Jerkface.

"Oh Remy, you do have quite the imagination. In case you were curious, you are currently being detained at the Glamerican Truth Extraction Facility in Prince Albert for crimes against Glamerica and its citizens."

"Crimes? What crimes? What have I done that's so deserving of the long arm of the law? And what the hell is a Prince Albert?"

Jacob opened the manila folder back up and removed a pocket calculator from his jacket. His fingers danced across the buttons of the adding machine as he read out the charges against me.

"Remy Delemme, citizen of Glamerica, you have been charged with the following crimes to the state of Glamerica and its New Quebecois allies: multiple counts of first-degree murder against Glamerican citizens, one count of murdering a Francophone — which carries the sentence of killing two Anglophones in New Quebec — as well as counts of grand theft auto, animal cruelty, sap lifting, terrorism, arson, public indecency, gun theft, the destruction of an endangered wasp nest and wearing a stolen false moustache, to name but a few. Would you like me to continue?"

"No, just let me know what the damages are and I'll settle up with you right now. Oh, and just for the record I still think I should have got that pizza for free. Your delivery woman was late."

Jacob stared at Remy for a few seconds before continuing his speech.

"Look Mr. Delemme, the crimes you have been charged with carry a maximum sentence of 583 years in a Glamerican Rehabilitation Camp by my count, and that's only if we don't allow the New Quebecers to string you up. Do you really want to spend the rest of your days behind bars?"

Sigh, this guy is playing some serious pizza hardball.

"This is going to cost more than twenty-four dollars and fifty cents, isn't it?"

Jacob exhaled smoke rings into the air for a few seconds before responding to me.

"Perhaps we can make an arrangement, Remy. Like I said, I think we're going to be friends. It isn't every day a man eludes one of our country's best profilers and detectives for as long as you did. It's impressive. We could use a man of your talents."

"How did you know about my talent? And how will my salsa dancing help me out of this mess?"

Jacob burst out laughing then grinned mischievously.

"We're definitely going to be friends, Remy. I like a man that knows how to dance," Jacob said as he removed a document and a brown envelope from his folder.

"This, Remy," Jacob said as he motioned to the document, "is how you will get out of this mess. This is your ticket to freedom."

"Great. Can I have it? We really don't have a lot of time. Rose is expecting me home soon."

"This is a non-negotiable deal. It will grant you pardons for all of the crimes you have committed in return for a few errands we need you to run for the good of our country. Agree to run these errands, and upon successful completion, you will have your freedom. I'm assuming you know how to follow a list, yes?"

I looked at Jacob and smiled.

"We're going to be good friends, Jacob."

30 Days Later...

Detective Gray sat in front of his living room television, grim-faced, as he watched Glamerica's Prime Minister address the people in what could be the start of The Third World War.

"My fellow Glamericans, we are under attack from the terrorist organization known as Nations Against Glomitrox. Several nations with direct ties to N.A.G. have begun fuelling weapons of mass destruction which they intend to fire on our great nation if I do not surrender myself for alleged crimes against humanity. Do not believe their propaganda. Our nuclear strikes on Paris, Moscow, Hong Kong, Tokyo, Berlin and Rome were pre-emptive strikes meant to protect our fair nation. We were completely within our rights to defend our homeland, especially after the underhanded assault on the City of Regina by unknown assailants that claimed thousands of lives. This unwarranted aggression towards our fair nation will not go unchecked. Any nation that supports the terrorist activities of

N.A.G. should consider this broadcast a final warning. Glamerica demands that all countries cease any plans for hostile actions against our fine state, or we will have no choice but to launch a full nuclear strike on all non-Glamerican soil.

Any Glamericans trained on how to survive a nuclear strike are to go door-to-door immediately and show their fellow citizens how to properly hide under a desk. This is Prime Minister Harper Day signing off. Good night and Glam bless."

The chill crawling up Gray's spine as he watched the Prime Minister give his address was broken by the sound of his cellphone ringing. Gray answered the call immediately.

"Boss, did you catch that shit the P.M. just said?" Crump asked.

"Yeah," Gray replied.

"End of the fuckin' world, boss."

"Maybe, rookie. But maybe not."

"What can we do to stop it? I mean, I don't really feel like just sitting on my thumbs and waiting for the apocalypse."

"Me neither, kid. And we won't. We're going to find the one man responsible for all of this."

"So, what's our next move?"

"We find Remy Delemme."

Author's Note

Staring at a finished version of this book fills me with a combination of joy, relief and anxiety. The end of this project has been a long time coming. I began this journey back in the winter of 2004, while attending Acadia University in Wolfville, Nova Scotia. It, not unlike Remy's adventure, started with a dream. I awoke from a bizarre dream at five in the morning and felt an overwhelming need to write about it. This is how Remy was born. I had so much fun writing about him that I continued to write about him for eight straight months. By the following December, my adventure with Remy had turned into a quick-and-dirty novella. That was ten years ago.

Getting to this point in my fiction writing has involved overcoming a variety of hurdles in my life – financial, health and otherwise – and it wouldn't have happened without the support I received from family and friends.

I am almost at a loss as to where to start my thanks and praise. But since I'm no fool, I'll start with my wife, Cristine.

Cristine has always been there to offer me whatever support I need to keep this book moving forward. From sitting down with me and brainstorming fun ideas for the book, to proofreads, critiques and marketing ideas, she has been involved in almost every aspect of this book. I have no doubt that this book is exponentially better because of her input.

Cristine, your constant pushing of me to accept nothing less than my best efforts when it comes to the overall quality of the book has taught me to expect more from myself as a writer and a person, and I'm eternally grateful for that. I love you, baby.

I also want to thank my mother and father, Jim and Violet, for all their support over the years and their assistance with helping me make this dream a reality. Dad, thank you for believing that even my craziest ideas might be attainable and for pushing me to chase my dreams. And Mom, thanks for constantly pushing for me to finish what I start from a young age.

Special thanks go out to my good friends Pj Monfero and Dan Zrobok. To Pj, thanks for taking the time to create all the fantastic drawings inside the book and the amazing cover art (sorry for all the re-designs); and Dan, thanks for keeping my author website alive, years after I had long forgotten about it.

To all my other friends that helped support me over the years through all of my crazy adventures I say, thank you.

Last but certainly not least, I must thank all the people who worked on the novel and did their part to make this book the most entertaining read it could be. To my editors Rosanne Lake, Alicia Androich and *Writer's Digest* line crtiquer Jack Adler, I say thanks for all of your assistance in cleaning up my book and making it a more enjoyable experience for its future readers.

About the Author

Andrew Snook is a professional writer and editor based in his hometown of Mississauga, Ontario. His passion for absorbing Canadian culture has fuelled his love for travelling across the country. He has only one goal in mind when writing fiction, and that is to make Canadians laugh out loud at inappropriate moments while shooting some sort of beverages out of their noses. Preferably, something not acidic. He's caring like that.

Printed in Canada